KID*NAPPED

Joyce M. Wilson

INFINITY
PUBLISHING.COM

ISBN 0-7414-5470-X

Published by:

INFI∞ITY
PUBLISHING.COM

*1094 New DeHaven Street, Suite 100
West Conshohocken, PA 19428-2713
Info@buybooksontheweb.com
www.buybooksontheweb.com
Toll-free (877) BUY BOOK
Local Phone (610) 941-9999
Fax (610) 941-9959*

Printed in the United States of America

Published August 2009

Chapter One

As the dust settled around the coach and the heat of the day made its way through the doors and windows I tried desperately to recognize something of this land. I was born here, but I had left at an early age. Could it be possible that I recognized the flow of the hills, and the sound of the river running wild down the canyon? No, I answered myself, just wishful thinking.

It had been a long ride from Stonehigh, Vermont. It had been almost 1,500 miles. I had traveled day and night and the stops had been few and far between. But it's never enough when your bones are aching and your feet are so swollen that you can't put your shoes on. You can't believe that it's your body. I have always worked hard and this sitting for days just doesn't feel good.

The stage coach driver pulled up to a spot off the road and unhitched the team of horses. These poor things had been going at a full pace for the last several hours and I was glad to see that the driver cared enough for these beautiful animals to let them rest and get a drink of water from the cool stream that flowed from the main river that we had been following for the past 2 days.

I took this time to slip my throbbing feet into the coolness of the water and immediately got a glimpse of what heaven must be like. Watching the ripples on the water and listening to the sound made that moment almost perfect. The hem of my dress was wet but I didn't care. I knew that it would be dry in a short time when we returned to the coach.

I was one of 4 passengers. Each of us was quiet and kept our thoughts to ourselves. Only every once in a while did a word leave someone's lips. It was as if they were all reading my thoughts. Privacy was very important to me. I would be the first to reach my destination and I could hardly contain myself. What a great name for a town 'Wild River Junction'. Even the name caused an excitement inside of me. Nebraska was a beautiful state.

I wondered if I would find my family still alive. I had no idea, only a deep sensation of hope. It had been 17 years since I had seen them, my beautiful mother and my tall handsome father. They had married later in life than most people. Mother had been a seamstress and had come to Nevada in an attempt to make a new life for herself after her first husband had been killed in a mining accident. She had built herself a lucrative business and was content with her life. Then one day a new Sheriff came into town and as mother always said to me, "I had believed that my life was perfect but I was wrong. Only after I married your father and you were born did I fine true happiness." Daddy had left his Sheriff's position soon after they were married and they had purchased a section of land just 5 miles out of town. Together they had worked the land and built their house. Oh, I had loved them both so deeply. Our life had been perfect, or so I remembered. Maybe – just maybe… Oh what is the use in thinking about it? In just 12 hours I will be there and I will see for myself.

Feeling a new energy from the cool water and the little walk I took down the road I returned to the coach anxious to face the last part of my journey.

* * * *

As the coach pulled into town I marveled at how Wild River Junction had grown. Last time I had seen it there had been only 5 or 6 businesses on the main street, but now there were so many more and several homes had been built around the outskirts.

The driver handed down my bag and directed me to Rose MacAffee's. "The best Boarding House in town," he told me. A young boy appeared out of nowhere and offered to carry my bag for me for a nickel. I smiled to myself and thought about the times that I would have done the same thing just to earn some money. I acknowledged his offer and with the energy of the young he took off down the street and, not having my land legs yet, I found it hard to keep up with him. I yelled to him to slow down. He found it hard to contain himself, but within a short time we approached a lovely home. Freshly painted and the yard full of flowers climbing over the fence and grass seemingly extra green with the damp ground. The sign in the window stated that this was Rose MacAffee's Boarding House and that there were rooms available to rent. On the front porch the young lad deposited my suitcase and turned to me with a great smile. I reached into my purse and presented him with his asked for reward.

As I knocked I heard the scuff of feet hurrying towards the door. Upon it being opened I was greeted with a wonderful smile and a warm greeting.

"Hello dear, I'm Mrs. MacAffee. If your needing a room, well then you are in luck I have two vacant at this moment." Mrs. MacAffee was the perfect picture of a beloved grandmother. Soft, cuddly, rounded with white hair.

"Mrs. MacAffee, my name is Sierra Martin." As I extended my hand it was received with a warm smile.

"Do come in dear and I'll show you to your room. How long do you think you'll be with us?"

"I honestly don't know yet Mrs. MacAffee. I'm considering starting a business here but as yet I don't know for sure. Would there be a problem if my stay was indefinite?"

"Oh. My gracious no! I always look forward to people who stay a long time. That means I've made a new friend."

I followed her up the carpeted stairs and down a wood paneled hall. She stopped at a dark colored oak door marked #7 and inserted a key in the lock. The door sprang open and I was amazed at the beauty of this room. A large double bed sat in the middle of the room against the wall. This wall faced the display of a bay window covered with lace curtains and a wardrobe set against the far wall. A dresser was just behind the open door and a pitcher was set in a gold crested basin ready for washing the dust of the day away. Everything was so neat and clean. It seemed to say "Welcome". I peeked outside the window and was greeted by the green mountains in the distance.

"I hope that this will be satisfactory my dear".

"Oh, Mrs. MacAffee, it's just wonderful. I know I'll be very comfortable here".

"If you need anything, just let me know and I'll try to help. Oh, by the way, breakfast is served in the dining room at 6 a.m., lunch at noon, and dinner at 6 p.m. I don't ask my guests to get all dressed up, but I do expect them to look clean and decent. Your towels are in the bottom drawer. The bathroom is at the end of the hall. I'll leave you now and see you at dinner."

"Thank you Mrs. MacAffee. I look forward to it".

As she left the room and quietly closed the door I figured I had a few hours before dinner and decided that I would look around this town that I had known before but did not recognize. Besides, I wanted to hire a horse and buggy and go for a drive out to the farm. But, maybe I should wait until tomorrow for the drive. I needed more time for that visit and knew that I needed to be rested and calm for whatever I would find there. As I unpacked my few belongings I began to realize that I was bone tired. I'm sure it was caused from all that jostling in the coach for all those hours and I never could sleep even at night. Suddenly the bed seemed very inviting and I couldn't resist trying out the soft feather mattress. "I'm just going to rest for a little while," I told myself. I thought about removing my clothing and washing my tired, dirty body, but it was too much of an effort to get back off the bed. I could hear the rustle of the breeze as it came in the open window and I opened my eyes, just a little and saw the lace curtains dancing. A bird outside the window was singing its song and it seemed to be saying "Welcome home, Sierra."

The first sensation I felt was heaviness in my body. I tried to open my eyes but they were too heavy to respond. I drifted back into the oblivion of sleep and my dreams were of a young child playing with her dolls and then a cold fear crept into her eyes as she hugged her toy to her. She backed away from someone and as she did I was suddenly falling into space and cried out that I wanted to help her but she was out of reach. I awoke with a start. At first I couldn't recognize my surroundings. The room was so strange, but then I remembered. A soft glow of daylight was on the horizon and peeked through the windows. I realized that I had slept all night. Poor Mrs. MacAffee would probably wonder why I had not appeared at the dinner table last night. Dinner! I'd missed it. No wonder I felt so hungry.

Pouring the water from the pitcher into the china bowl I washed myself and took a clean, but wrinkled day dress from the wardrobe. I knew that I had to put up with a few irritating things before I was settled. I carefully smoothed out the sheets and pulled the beautiful quilt up to the headboard. There was something very serene about this room. As I glanced around I felt that my life was just beginning.

* * * *

Walking down the softly carpeted stairs I could smell breakfast cooking. My mouth watered and at that moment I heard my stomach say "Wow!" I followed the aroma and passed through a parlor then entered the dining room. A large table was set for ten people. The arrangement of the dishes, silverware, glasses and even flowers on the table were a sight to behold. No one but Mrs. MacAffee would have set a table so elegantly in a boarding house.

"Mrs. Rathburn! My dear I hope you're alright? I was worried about you when you missed supper last night. I do hope everything was to your liking."

"Everything was perfect Mrs. MacAffee. I'm sorry I missed dinner, but I was so exhausted from my trip that I'm afraid my short afternoon nap turned into a long overnight sleep. And, please Mrs. MacAffee, call me Sierra."

"Sit here Sierra. Most of the other boarders have had their breakfast and gone to work. A few of them haven't seen fit to get out of bed yet. I have a couple of people who do not work, but as long as they can pay their rent, I have no qualms about that".

I made quite a pig of myself regarding breakfast, but it was so delicious. Eggs the way I like them, slabs of ham, sausages, potatoes and then the most delectable platter of biscuits and gravy. The coffee was steaming hot. "If this was breakfast, what in the world would supper be like?" I thought to myself.

And so my first day in Wild River Junction began. Quietly, peacefully, a lovely place to stay and a full stomach. What more could a person ask for? Well, I suppose a lot more, but for me, for now, this was perfect.

* * * *

The buggy I rented from the old livery man creaked and groaned as I urged the horse forward. That this poor creature

6

had traveled many miles was very evident. However I was promised "a nice ride and if anything happened the horse knew his way home". Of course I could not remember exactly the route to the farm, but I could follow the trail that seemed to have been made with years of use by wagons and horses. There seemed to be a lot of grass and weeds on the trail and my heart was heavy with thought. That meant if people were living at the farm they had not traveled this way in a long time.

Watching the hawk fly upward into the sky I felt akin to him. I may not be flying, but I feel as if I'm soaring and the sky's the limit. I felt a freedom that I have never felt. I urged the poor horse into a trot and let the wind blow through my hair. "Please God," I prayed "don't let this be a dream. I'll need all the help you can give me. There is a little someone counting on both of us to give her a good life."

As we passed over the miles, I began to notice little things, like the little stream that I had crossed over when riding into town with daddy on the old wagon. There was that old craggy tree lifting its branches up to heaven like two arms pleading. Then a dip in the road and as I pulled to the top of the hill, there it was, home, or what I had called home for the first five years of my life.

I entered below the battered archway that had once proudly announced that this was the 'Rathburn Ranch'. The sign was setting on the ground. The wind and rain had dulled the luster to an almost unreadable statement. The sorrow that I felt when I saw the house and the condition of the property brought tears to my eyes. It was very evident that no one lived here anymore and hadn't in a long, long time.

I pulled the horse up to the creaking gate that used to be part of a white picket fence that had surrounded a true Garden of Eden. No more are the Hollyhocks stretching up. No more the sumptuous beds of Chrysanthemums, Hyacinths and Carnations smiling at me. The green grass had long since died and a sea of weeds had taken its place. How long, I wondered had this been abandoned.

Carefully I picked my way across the porch to the front door. It was hanging by one hinge, and even that looked precarious. I entered the old house and gasped with surprise to see mom's old rocking chair setting on a bare wood floor. Missing was the rug she had made. She had spent hours braiding yards and yards of material to make the rug that had set under her chair. The table and chairs that we had sat at for our meals sat bare and covered with dust. We used to sit here and work on which ever projects we had going at that time. Mom would sew her quilts or do her mending. There was always something she had to patch or darn. Pop would work on his paperwork or clean his pipe and I would be reading or writing. I hadn't started school yet, but mom had made sure that I would be well prepared when I did. What wonderful time's mom and I had as we would sit there after dinner in the evenings and work on my lessons, learning how to read and write and do my sums. There was always laughter in this house and lots of love. I was never very attentive to the lessons. I had more important things on my mind, like catching that old frog in the pond or taking my dog, Scotty, for a walk or helping daddy with the chores. Poor momma! How she tried. I loved her so.

Her big black kettle still set on the hearth, but now, instead of the wonderful smell of her stew bubbling on the fire, there was nothing but cobwebs and spiders. I walked across the room and entered what had been their bedroom. The old brass bed still set there with the covers and pillows still in place. A musty odor filled the room and I looked towards the window and saw the tattered remnants of mom's fine lace curtains that she had sat and crochet with her own hands. The family bible was still lying on a table beside the bed and I reached down and pulled it from amongst the webs that covered it. I blew the dust off and opened it. On the first page were the names of George and Sadie Rathburn. Then beneath was written Sierra Rose Rathburn born on January

21, 1815. There was another entry that I did not understand. It said Matthew Barnes Rathburn, born August 31, 1803. Who was Matthew Barnes Rathburn? Did they have a son after I left? No, they couldn't have. According to the dates, he's 12 years older than I am.

Pondering all of this I carried the Bible with me into the main room and began to climb up into the loft. This had been my room. As I climbed high enough to see, I found a much larger bed occupying the space where my little bed had been. No sign of the frills mom had put around the coverlet or at the window. There was just plain dark brown material. I caught a cry in my throat. There was nothing left that had been mine in this room. I ran down the stairs and out into the sunlight. I sank down onto the ground and cried. Frustration had a hold of me and I cried and sobbed from all of the pent up feelings that I had buried inside of me for all these years. My parents were gone! They were probably dead. How could it be, it just wasn't fair. And who is this Matthew person?

Chapter 2

Sitting in my room I kept revisiting the day. What could have happened to my parents that everything they had owned was still in that house? It was as if they had suddenly fallen off the face of the earth. And who was the man whose name was next to mine in the Bible? I guess that will be found out when my questions are answered.

At supper that night I met the rest of Mrs. MacAffee's boarders. As I had approached the dining room, I was aware of the buzz of people talking, an occasional laugh and the clatter of dishes. Nervously I entered the room. I wasn't at ease with strangers and I was about to meet several of them.

"Oh! Mrs. Martin. How good that you're joining us. Everyone, this is our newest boarder, Mrs. Sierra Martin. She'll be with us for quite a while. Now, while I get another dish of potatoes, please introduce yourselves, one at a time if you please, and Mrs. Martin, don't let Hank there give you any guff. He's the tease of this group."

Introductions were made all the way around. There were two ladies and five men. I was warmly greeted and felt immediately at ease with this group. You could instantly feel the camaraderie between them. They had evidently known each other for a long time. I was looking forward to being as comfortable and at ease as they seemed to be with each other.

As soon as the cordial hellos were said, the clatter of the dishes the talking and the laughter were back.

"Mrs. Martin, were do you hale from?" The man on my right politely asked.

"Oh I lived for a number of years in Stonehigh, Vermont".

"And what made you leave that part of the country?" The man on my left asked.

"I just felt that I needed to see something of this country before I got too old to do it. I have always wanted to visit this area."

"Now Mule, you and Hank quit asking Mrs. Martin so many questions, and let her eat. I swear you two are the nosiest people I know. Here dear, have some of these potatoes. They are my specialty. I add a little butter and parsley to them. They are guaranteed to melt in your mouth. Go on now, eat up."

The friendly atmosphere was like a balm on my heart. I began to face my problem with a more positive attitude and decided that I would put today behind me just for the rest of the evening. Tomorrow was a new day. There was time enough to start my new life.

After dinner I was invited to join the others in the parlor. This room was large and had several plush armchairs set in individual groups. There was a table between two other chairs and on the top of it a chess game was laid out. It looked as if a game was in progress. The warmth from the fireplace spread through the room and each of the others went to their special places. Martha and Violet sat beside the fire. A beautiful brocade settee was placed in such a way that a conversation was easy to hold with anyone else in the room. Martha had brought some needle point with her, and Violet had her knitting. Mac and Virg seated themselves at the chess table and began contemplating their moves. A piano in the corner called to me and I asked if it was permissible to play. They all chorused encouragement and so I began to play, quietly.

Piano! What an escape it had been for me during those terrible years. He had never known that I was learning it. If he had known how much it meant to me he would have never have let me go to William Windsor's house again. It would never make up for the terrible things that I was expected to submit to with Mr. Windsor. But my reward was learning to play. It had all begun with that beautiful baby grand piano.

The big red door opened slowly. I had never seen a door like it before. In my ten year old mind it was a wonder to behold. Glancing up, up, up, I got my first look at William Windsor. A very tall man. He had eyes that sparkled and a smile that told me that he was someone special.

"Well! What do we have here? Why it's a beautiful ray of sunshine standing on my door step. Thank you for coming by to visit with me young lady. And what is your name?"

"Sierra Rose Rathburn, sir"

"My goodness what a beautiful name. Do come in. I have been waiting for you. Did Mr. Ward just leave you there on the step?"

"Yes sir."

"Did he tell you why you are here today?"

"He only told me to be good and do whatever you say for me to do."

"Well, come in and let me take your coat."

"What you gonna do with my coat?"

"Just hang it over this chair so that it will be ready for you when you leave."

"Oh! Thank you."

"Mr. Ward tells me that you are very good at tidying up around the house. Is that true?"

"Yes sir. I always like to put things away."

"Well I have need of someone to tidy up my library for me. Do you think you can do it?"

"Yes sir."

"Come this way then and we will get started." He talked funny and I was to learn later that he had grown up in London. He was a retired professor from the University.

I followed him down the dingy hall and at the third door to the left we entered into a room that was bigger than any I had ever seen. The place was a mess. It looked as if a wind had taken hold of everything on the shelves and then dumped them all over the floor, tables and any other flat surface.

Although I was ten, I had always been able to hold my own when it came to learning... mom had given me the basics. Even though I never went to school, I was able to teach myself from necessity. I don't believe that Carl knew just how much I had learned.

"Let us start in this corner of the room and work our way around to the fireplace."

We spent the next two hours picking up a book and dusting it off and then putting it in a special pile that Mr. Windsor had determined. Finally he suggested that he make us a cup of tea and then we would call it a day. I was to return to his house this same time next week. He hinted that the money he was paying Carl for my labor was well worth it.

It was about three weeks later that I began to get that sticky feeling up my spine. I had been climbing up a ladder to put some books onto the shelf when I realized that Mr. Windsor was standing directly under me. I felt myself flush as I looked down, knowing that he could see up my dress. I quickly came down the ladder and walked over to another pile of books to be dusted. He followed me and very gently took the cloth from my hand.

"Such a pretty little hand. What a shame that it is exposed to all this dirt and grime."

He lifted my hand and turned it over. He brushed a wisp of a kiss on my palm.

"You have very exciting hands Sierra. I love the way they feel. I like to watch you work with them. They are meant to bring extreme pleasure. Have you ever had extreme pleasure Sierra?

"I don't think so sir."

"Would you like to have extreme pleasure?"

"I don't know what you are talking about."

"Oh Sierra! My sweet, beautiful little thing. There are so many pleasures waiting out there for you. We may have to start with just a few small ones before you find the extreme one."

"I don't understand Mr. Windsor."

"Hasn't Mr. Ward taught you any of the pleasures?"

"No sir. Just to mind him or he'll beat me."

"Oh my precious child! Then I will take it upon myself to teach you. But we must never tell him, or else he might beat you again. Come here and sit in this chair. That's right.

Now one of the first things you have to learn is that in order to receive pleasure, you must learn to give it first. Do you want to learn Sierra?"

"I guess so, but I don't really understand."

"Well then let me show you."

And, standing before me he slowly began unbuttoning the front of his trousers. As each button snapped open I felt my heart stand still and I couldn't breathe. I knew that what was about to happen was wrong, I didn't know why I felt that way, but I knew it wasn't right. His trousers slipped down his legs and stayed at his knees. The pants underneath his *trousers were silky and shiny. He unbuttoned them and slipped them down. I looked down onto a protruding arm-like being.*

"Have you ever seen one of these before Sierra?"

"No sir."

"It is one of the things that brings great pleasure. It's called a penis. Do you want to touch it?"

"No sir."

"Yes you do my love. This is your first lesson. You will give me great pleasure if you will touch it."

I reached out but before I knew what was happening my hand pulled its self back.

"No, I don't want to touch it."

"Of course you do. It won't hurt you. It will feel so good. Please, Sierra. I'll give you a special reward if you will do as I say."

My fingertips found their way onto the appendage. Hot-sticky-hard.

"That's my girl. Now put your finger around it and rub. That's good. Oh yes that is so very good."

His breathing came faster and faster and suddenly, into my hand there came a sticky white substance.

"My wonderful girl! You have brought me much pleasure today. Thank you. Now are you ready for your reward? You have stated several times that you wish you could play the piano. Well as a treat I will teach you. Then every week when you are here we will give each other many pleasures!"

I entertained my fellow boarders for about an hour and then amidst thank yous and requests not to stop, I politely told them that I would be happy to play any evening we were together. At that, I left the room and silently walked up the stairs. Sitting on the chair beside the window I scanned the picture perfect view of the hills. Almost dark, the deep purple of the hills were making shadows that looked unreal.

If the people I met tonight are an example of the town's residents, I feel that I have come to the right place to find my new life.

Walking over to my dresser and opening the top drawer, I pulled out a journal and began to write down all of the events of the day. For as long as I could remember I have kept an account of my daily activities. Sometime, when I was with him I was only able to use scraps of paper, but since I began life on my own I have been able to use a true journal book. Someday, when I am stronger, I'll read all that I have written down over the years.

After my entries were made and my journal tucked safely away for the night, I brought to the small night table another note book. This one held all of the notes that I had made regarding my new life. I wanted to open a store for ladies only. I had always pictured an inviting front window with lace and frills displayed in such a way that the passing female could not resist entering my establishment. Saving every penny I could over the past several years I felt that I could at least start my shop on a small scale and then expand it as I acquired the means to do so.

Tomorrow would be the day that I would look around town for the best location available for my store, and at the same time, try to find out what I could about my parents and their home. I wondered if it was for sale. Settling on my bed my mind was racing with a thousand thoughts. Not an inducement to falling asleep but none the less relaxing and before I realized it I was slipping into that special world of oblivion and dreams. Upon waking, long into the night, I realized that a cool breeze was blowing across me. I snuggled down deeper into the feathery bed and slipped back into oblivion.

* * * *

At breakfast the next morning I made a mental note that I had better stop eating three meals a day at Mrs. MacAffee's or I would be my own first customer in my shop by buying larger clothes. How many times in the past had I been near to starving and decided that should I ever be in the position to eat any time, or as much as I wanted I would make a pig of myself? Our situations change the wants of our lives.

Waiting for an opportunity to talk to Mrs. MacAffee, I slowly sipped my last cup of coffee. Only Mule, Hank and Virg were eating breakfast and they were almost done. Their work today was to search for a new section of land. They were surveyors, and had been contracted by the government to survey a section of land at a position that the government was planning to put a railroad line across. No wonder they all looked so tanned. They spent many hours out in the open. When they were finished with their breakfast they had gathered all their paraphernalia and left the boarding house. I waited for Mrs. MacAffee to enter the dining room to clear the table. As the door to the kitchen swung open and she entered I couldn't help but wonder if she slept with that smile on her lovely face.

"I hope you had enough to eat Sierra?"

"Oh! More than enough. I'm going to have to slow down some when it comes to eating your wonderful food, Mrs. MacAffee."

"Oh! You are so kind, but then you need fattening up a little. I hate to see any of my tenants looking scrawny."

"Mrs. MacAffee, do you have a couple of minutes that we could talk."

"Certainly I do. Martha and Violet are the only ones that have not eaten yet and they never come down until the very last minute. Those two love their beds. They are the last to go to bed at night and they are the last to get up in the mornings. Let me pour us both a cup of coffee and we can talk."

She brought the delicate china coffee pot to the table and filled our cups with the steaming liquid.

"Now my dear, what can I help you with?"

I told her about my life in Stonehigh, Vermont. How I had been an assistant to a women who had a shop that catered to women only, and that I had decided to try and start my own shop in another town. I had known someone that used to visit here in Wild River Junction and they were very fond of it. That was the reason that I chose it to make my attempt at the store. I told her that I was looking for a building that I could use. I didn't much care if I had to repair an old building. If remodeling was approved then I would be able to make the shop look the way I have always dreamed of it being.

"Well let's see dear… there is a building at the end of the main street. It used to be an eating place, but the owners couldn't cook worth a darn, so nobody went there and they went broke. A couple of old codgers they were. Figured that they had cooked all their lives in the mining camps and so they had to be good at it. A shame really, they were nice old gents. They left this area and went back to the camps. It would probably take a lot of work to fix it up, but the location is really perfect for what you want. I believe that Molly Howard, the owner of the Wild River Saloon owns it. You might take a walk down to the hotel and see her about noon time. That's usually when she has lunch there."

"I knew I could count on you Mrs. MacAffee. I really appreciate your help. I'll make a point of being at the hotel by noon. By the way, have you ever heard of a man by the name of Matthew Rathburn?"

"No. I don't believe so. The name does sound familiar but I can't say that I know of him. Oh! Wait a minute, there used to be a family that lived just outside of town by the name of Rathburn. I never knew them, but I just heard about them from the towns folk. Whether his name was Matthew or not, I don't know. You might ask Molly when you see her. She's been here for over 20 years."

"Thanks, I just might. I came across the name yesterday and I was curious as to who he was, or is."

* * * *

Feeling anxious to get a look at the building that Mrs. MacAffee had told me about, I went to my room and put on my coat and hat. I glanced over at the table beside the bed and saw the old Bible that I had taken from the Rathburn's house. I felt guilty about having it, and yet I had to have something that made me feel closer to them. I will solve this mystery, I promised myself.

I walked out into the clean, warm sunshine. The street was busy with the bustle of people going their ways. I knew that to find the main street I needed to walk two blocks, turn left and that would bring me to the street I was looking for. Two blocks on that old wooden sidewalk with my boots clunking and my skirt swishing was a breath of fresh air. People that I passed nodded to me and a couple of gentlemen tipped their hats. My! A really friendly atmosphere. I began to think that maybe I could really pull this off.

Walking down the main street I passed a barber shop, a store that sold only fruits and vegetables and a small coffee shop. The general store was across the street and I was curious as to the merchandise it carried. Carefully I crossed the muddy street and entered Bellman's Country Store. I must say that the merchandise was displayed with flair. Whoever had done this window had a real sense of eye catching appeal. The food goods were displayed on my left and the notions on my right. Jars of candy set up by the counter in colors of the rainbow. How they must have tantalized the young folk who came into the store on an errand for mom or dad. Large barrels of flour and beans and coffee beans set in a trio in the middle of the room. A black pot belly stove set at the other end. The shelves behind the counter were stocked with all kinds of non perishable goods. Bolts of different types of material were displayed on the shelves on the right hand side. All colors, designs and textures. Spools of different colored thread were stacked one on top of the other forming a pyramid. Jars of buttons were displayed. I knew that if my little shop was to be successful I would somehow have to convince the owner of this place to sell me all of his "Womanly" goods. I smiled, telling myself, "Let's not get ahead of ourselves. I'd better see this shop first. I can come back at a later time."

"Is there something I can get for your?" a young girl asked as I crossed to the door.

"Thank you, no. I'm new in town and I was curious as to what goods you handled in here. You have a very lovely place. I am certain that I will be back."

I quickly exited the shop and continued with my trek down the main street. The further down the street I walked I noticed that there were many select stores. A silversmiths, a book store, an assayers office. A bank and next door a sign over the entranceway stated that Bill Trexel, Attorney At Law was now practicing. It seemed to be a very neat assemblage of working people that were trying to make a living. I felt encouraged by all of this.

Finally, reaching the end of the street, I saw the empty building. It wasn't on the left or right of the street. The street came to an end at the shops door. It was very evident that the building hadn't seen a coat of paint or any care in a long time. The large windows were intact. No cracks. Just a fine film of dirt from the outside and a layer of spider webs from the inside. I tried to peer into the building, but found it hard to see anything. I walked around the building and paced it off as I walked. I counted sixteen feet across the front and forty feet down the side. Hmm! Not a bad size. I should be able to have a display room and a back room for personal attention needed. How will the towns women take to being able to buy a ready made dress and try it on before they purchase it? There seemed to be plenty of window space. I was happy about that. I'm a firm believer in having window displays that will coax clients into the shop.

You know that itchy feeling you get that deep down tells you, this is it. Go for it. I tried to calm my excitement, but found it hard to do. "Easy girl! You don't even know if you can have this building. Wait until you talk to the owner. Then celebrate." Talking to myself had become a habit over the years. Sometimes it would be the only voice I would hear for days at a time.

Mrs. MacAffee had said that the saloon owner was the one that owned this building too. I've been inside a saloon a time or two in my life, but it had never been related to a pleasant experience. "I remember once… never mind forget that. It's time to move on."

I didn't remember passing the saloon as I had made my walk down the main street. I guess that I must have missed it.

Glancing once more at the empty building and seeing it as it could be with a little care, I walked back down the street towards Mrs. MacAffee's house. Paying more attention this time I was aware of all the shops I passed. There was not one that even resembled a saloon. I decided to go into the general store once more and I knew I could get directions. I found the same pleasant girl in the store and when I asked her about the whereabouts of the saloon, she almost chocked. "Are you sure you want to go to the saloon?"

"Yes, please I would appreciate your giving me the directions."

"Well, when you go down to the bottom of the street, where the empty store is, turn left and go down that street for about two blocks. You'll see it on your left. It's called the 'Wild River Saloon'.

I thanked her and walked back down towards "My" store. Once again I got that itchy feeling.

* * * *

I could hear the music coming from inside before I even saw the building. The same old tunes played on the same old type rinky-dink piano. Some things never change. There were several horses tied up to the hitching post out front and I could also hear laughter coming from inside. I knew that a woman walking into a saloon alone, takes a chance, but I was bound and determined that I was not going to let this stop me from talking to Molly Howard.

By the time the swinging doors had come to a stop, every eye in the place was on me. I'm thinking to myself that I should have worn more layers of clothes. I felt that everyone was stripping me down to nothing.

Trying to show a confident air I walked over to the bar tender and asked him if Molly Howard was there.

"We 'aint hiring right now", he said, "but come back in a couple of weeks. We're expecting a cattle drive crew to come through then."

"I'm not looking for work, thank you. I just want to speak to Molly Howard."

"What do you want to talk to her about?"

"I'm sorry, but this is a personal business matter. Now is she here or not?"

"Don't get uppity with me girl."

"I'm sorry; I really don't mean to be rude. I just need to speak to Miss Howard."

The sound of rustling taffeta came from behind me and a very pleasant, attractive lady came into view.

"Is there a problem Boots?" she asked the bartender.

"This here gal wants to talk to you about a personal business matter."

"Well then Boots, maybe we should just talk to her then. Hello, my name is Molly Howard. Come over and sit down with me. Would you like a drink?"

I thanked her for her thoughtfulness, but declined the offer. I have never been able to appreciate the effect that alcohol has on a person. I've seen too many problems come from drinking.

"Miss Howard, my name is Sierra Martin. I'm here to talk to you about that store you own on Main Street the one at the end of the road. I heard that it used to be a restaurant."

"Oh yes! Blackie and Spade tried to make a go of it. Poor guys! They didn't know the first thing about business, let alone about cooking. It didn't last very long."

"Well, I'm new in town and I plan on staying for a long time, possibly for many years. I've been trained in finer apparel for ladies and I want to open a shop here in Wild River. I walked around town today and found your shop. I believe it would be perfect for my wares."

"Wow! I don't know. Are you sure you want it? It'll take a lot of work to get it cleaned up. Do you have the funding to get the work done that's needed and get your stock supplies?"

"Yes I'm sure that I do. I'm very handy when it comes to repairs and painting. I have also been trained in decorating for the best effect of my wares."

We sat and talked about the store, my style of merchandise and just about everything else. Before our visit was over we had become friends and I had her permission to proceed forward with my dream. She gave me the key to the building and a warm handshake as we parted company.

Unlocking the door was so exciting. She was right. There was a lot to be done, but I got right down to the planning and calculating. There was even a small room in the back of the shop that I could convert into a bedroom for myself. That would mean that I could save money by living in the shop. I knew that I would hate to give up that wonderful room at Mrs. MacAffee's, but there will be time later for little luxuries, maybe even big luxuries.

Chapter 3

And so my days passed quickly. I had so much to do! I began by hiring a young man to help me with the heavy jobs.

Pat Grady was his name and he was a real treasure. He was 16 years old and a brute of a boy/man. He teetered on the brink of both of these. One minute excitable and quiet like a boy and then strong and alert like a man.

The first thing we did was to gut the inside of the building. We did it carefully so as not to destroy any of the materials that we could use again. Actually, we managed to save a lot. Then we began the rebuilding one step at a time and with great care. It soon began to take the shape of the shop that I had always dreamed about.

The first part that was finished was my living quarters. It consisted of a small bed/sitting room and a tiny but usable kitchen. If I had tried to turn around in the bathroom I would never have made it. Not exactly a palace, but at least it was livable and it was mine.

Mrs. MacAffee was saddened when I told her that I would be leaving her house. She arranged a special dinner on that last night. All the tenants were there and we ate and laughed into the late night. I played one more time for them on the piano and then said my goodbyes. After finishing my packing I spent a restless night, tossing and turning. I was so excited and so just before dawn, I was up and in 'my Shop'. I was going to have Pat help to move my belongings later that day.

Each board that was nailed and each coat of paint that was applied was watching a dream come true. I had poured for hours over the catalogs that I had brought with me on my trip and now finally came the time for me to send in my order. I walked so proudly into the general store and at the mail window I gave Henry Bellman the envelope and happily paid for the postage.

"Mr. Bellman how long do you think that letter will take to reach its destination?"

"Several weeks, I would imagine Miss Martin. Why? Are you anxious for a reply?"

"You will never know how anxious Mr. Bellman."

I had talked to the general store owner the month before. I had explained to him about the plans I had made and what I had in mind for my shop. I had assured him that my line of ladies wear would not take too many sales from his store. He had explained to me, with a very red face and stumbling through words that he was uncomfortable to utter, that there were certain ladies items that he would just as soon not have to deal with. He seemed to be very relieved by the whole idea. I was so very happy about this. I did not want to start off on the wrong foot with a fellow merchant.

What seemed like years, but in essence was only a couple of months, the finishing touches of "Sierra's Finery For Women." was finished. I had decided on the name months ago while this was all just a dream. Now all I had to do was to wait for the coach to arrive that was delivering my 'finery' and I would be ready to open. Just thinking of all that lay ahead was exhilarating! It's not everyone that can realize a dream.

A couple of weeks later, Pat ran breathlessly into the store and announced that the coach was in and that I had a big shipment on board.

How lovingly I unpacked each item. Everything seemed to float on air as in a dream. Here it was. The rest of my life beginning and hopefully I could send for Annie just as soon as I started to make some money. The years had taught me to be tough and I was amazed when I felt tears sliding softy down my cheeks. Just anticipating what could be ahead of me verged on taking my breath away. This was so important. This little shop just had to work. I was betting mine and Annie's whole future on it.

The date was set for the opening of "Sierra's Finery For Women." I had spent hours writing out invitations to the women of Wild River Junction. I had passed them out while walking up and down the streets. I had made a special invitation for Molly Howard. She had replied that she would be happy to attend the opening, but she felt that her presence would hamper any of the "good" women from coming. However, she stated, if I could maybe let her come in the shop the evening before, she would be thrilled to attend the opening.

I had spent many hours talking to Molly about the shop and I had found her to be an honest genuine person. She had given me many suggestions regarding the displays and we had so many of the same thoughts about the items. I had become very attached to her. I had answered her letter by telling her that I would not have a special showing for her, that I would expect her to visit the shop during the specified hours and that if any of the women stayed away because Molly was there then that female was not wanted in my shop anyhow. Every woman that came in was going to be treated on an equal basis. Besides I doubted that I would find a finer woman than Molly.

The big day finally came. I was up at the crack of dawn and went around my displays and gently touched each and every one of them just to make sure that they were in the right position. There was the frilly nightgown draped over the wicker chair, the laced bloomers accented by the ribbons hanging down from the overhead decoration. There were bright pink boxes of undergarments in all the colors of the rainbow. Over by the register were the gloves. The hats were held up high by the heads of the wicker models, the feathers and the bows stately adorning the brims. Stockings and shawls peeked out from the glass display case. Shoes of various sizes stood at attention on the shelf. I had specialty boots for the garden or boots for riding and the newest specialty, a shoe just for inside the house. Warm and fuzzy fur would bring warmth to the wearer on a chilly day. A special display of a white organza nightgown and matching penoir decorated the window in the front. Hopefully people walking by would not be able to resist the temptation of the possibility that other lovely things could be on the inside of the shop. I had only ordered one of these organza sets. After all how many women living in little shack homes would want the lacy things? Not many I knew, but they looked so beckoning in the window. And there again who knows but that there might be more buyers than I thought. I could always order more if need be. Finally, satisfied that everything was as I wanted it, I put the sign in the window and announced that I was 'Open'.

It wasn't a crowd of people that entered within the next hour. There were a few stragglers every now and then. It was mostly women just looking. But I felt that at least they were there, and would be back. I served them little scones and tea and greeted each one with a smile. Toward mid-day, I heard the tinkle of the bell that was over the door as another customer entered. It was Molly. She had driven the two blocks from the saloon in a handsome horse and buggy. She was dressed in her best finery. Her dress was a cloud of yellow organdy that floated around her as she walked, her gloves the same shade and her hat finished off the outfit with a beautiful yellow feather surrounding the large brim. She was stunning. I appreciated her dressing up on this special day and I was so glad to see her. As she entered, the two people who had been in the shop seemed taken aback by her entrance. They looked as if they would like to find some place to run and hide. As Molly entered the shop, I greeted her with a peck on her cheek and told her how happy I was to see her. I then deliberately turned to the two ladies and asked them if they had ever met Molly Howard. They both quietly said no, so I introduced them and Molly reached out to shake their hands. I must admit it was a bit of a stiff handshake, but none the less it had happened.

How does one explain the pride and self confidence one feels when they have completed something they have dreamed about for years? These jittery, butterfly feelings inside me were so foreign. Could it be that at last I can live a life without shame, terror and poverty?

"Sierra! What a beautiful place you have here. There are so many lovely things. If I didn't know better I would believe I was in a small shop in Paris. Not that I have ever been to Paris, but I have a great imagination."

"Thank you Molly. I put a lot of effort into this place to make it somewhere that women would want to come to, if only to sit and chat for a while. Of course I would love for them to buy things too."

"I have no doubt that you will do very well. Now let me see, which of these two nightgowns shall I buy? The pink or the rose colored one?"

After wrapping up Molly's purchases I invited her to sit a while and have a cup of tea. While we were seated, two other ladies came into the store and I was able to talk them into trying on some of the dresses that were ready made. They were astounded that I had a place for them to enter for privacy so that they could try on the dresses.

"Beats taking them home with you and then finding out that you don't fit into them. Then you have to bring them back and exchange and probably have to do that a couple more times until you get the one that fits perfectly." This was stated by the elder of the women. "And the prices are very reasonable. I'll be back for more things in the future. I am so tired of buying my things through the catalog. They never send you the size that you want. Then you have to package it all up again and mail it away. It takes forever to get exactly what you want. By the way, my name is Helen Whitt. My husband is the mayor of Wild River Junction."

"Mrs. Whitt, I am so very happy to meet you. I hope that you and I will have a very pleasant relationship in the future. Please, come by and see me whenever you are in town. We can talk about what it is the women of this town desire from my kind of store."

"I would love to do that Mrs. Rathburn."

"Oh! Please, call me Sierra."

Mrs. Whitt gathered her skirts about her and swooped out the door. As she passed Molly she gave a friendly nod of acknowledgment. Her young friend followed, looking like a puppy dog following along.

"You can't make a better friend than old Helen." Molly stated, "She will be sure that all the women of Wild River hear about you. She's a good old girl at heart. Can't think why she puts up with that husband of hers though. He loves to pry into everything. Telling people that he has to because it is his responsibility as mayor to know everything that goes on. Heard tell that he's pretty touchy feely with the ladies too."

"I thought it was only women who were supposed to gossip and pry"

"Not in this case. Now Sierra, how about coming over to the saloon tonight and having dinner with me in the restaurant? We don't have any fancy food, but what we have will stick to your ribs. I really think we need to celebrate this first day of "Sierra's Finery For Women". I don't know about you, but I believe it has been a rousing success."

"I think I've done much better today than I had hoped for. I didn't make a million dollars this first day, but I sure made a couple of nice friends. Dinner would be wonderful, and I might even have a glass of wine."

"Done!", said Molly as she stepped up into her carriage. Setting her packages down beside her, she added "See you around seven then."

Chapter 4

I saw him out of the corner of my eye. The swinging doors parted and this rugged ape of a man appeared. He didn't look much worse than some of the men in the saloon and yet there was something about him that caused sparks to emanate from his frame. It seemed that everyone turned to watch him walk over to the bar. In a husky voice he ordered his choice of drink, and when served, the liquid was poured quickly down his throat. "One more, bar tender. This next one is for sipping." He turned then and slowly looked out across the saloon taking in the restaurant as well.

I was seated at a table in the back of the restaurant with Molly and we had just finished a very enjoyable dinner. We were working on a large serving of apple pie at the moment. "Molly! That was the best meal I've had since I left Mrs. MacAffee's. You two are bound and determined to put some meat on my bones. You are what I call hazardous to my health."

"Well honey, it's just that we want you to look as round and jolly as we do, that way we won't be embarrassed when we're with you. Now! How about another cup of coffee? Hey Boots! Bring over that coffee pot before we die of thirst over here."

It was at this instant that Molly saw the man at the bar. I could see a glimmer of recognition in her eyes, and yet, you could see that she wasn't so sure. She studied him for a couple of seconds, and as their eyes meet he broke into a big grin, she gave a loud "Halloo". As she rose from the table at the speed of lightening her chair clattered to the floor. In just an instant she was across the room and into the waiting arms of the grizzly character waiting for her with his arms out stretched. There was no doubt now. Molly knew exactly who he was.

"Oh my God, Matthew, I thought you would never come back here. Where have you been? How long are you going to stay? … and how come you never let anyone know what happened to you? I am so angry at you. But I am so glad to see you."

Even the distance from the table to where they were was not enough that I could not see the tears welling up in Molly's eyes. It was so very apparent that this was someone who was very special to her. Everyone in the place was sitting with a big grin on his or her face. You couldn't help it. Joy displayed like that just seems to ripple through a room and affects everyone.

"Well, Molly my love. Guess I have a lot to tell you, but I sure can't do it on an empty stomach. How about feeding me first?"

"Sure Matt. Lets go over here and I'll introduce you to a friend of mine that I seemed to have left all on her lonesome. Sierra, I am so sorry about that, but I just couldn't let this lug get out of here before I grabbed hold of him. Matt, this is my friend Sierra Martin." Matt extended his hand to me. I couldn't ever remember shaking hands with someone whose hands seemed so big and warm. "I am most happy to meet you Matt. You're evidently very important to Molly. It's nice to see her so happy."

"Matt and I go way back, Sierra. When I first came to Wild River he was a snot nosed kid trying to look up every petticoat he could find. He used to crawl under the sidewalks, just waiting for the women to walk across the spaces in the planks. But he stole my heart. Too bad he wasn't older, or better yet that I wasn't younger, we would have made a great combination. "

The next couple of hours seemed to flow without any sense of time. Matt explained to Molly that when his folks had died he just couldn't seem to settle down with any apparent goal in life. He was only 19 and didn't want to settle for just being a farmer. So he had left Wild River and roamed around the country. Sometimes he herded cattle. Sometimes he worked on sheep ranches. After several years he became acquainted with a couple of lawmen and tried his hand at keeping the peace. He seemed to find a niche in this old world then. He had been involved with the law for the past six years.

"You know Molly, being able to help improve people's life by keeping the law is a very rewarding job. But! Can you believe I am beginning to get a burr under my saddle about being a farmer! I guess that at my age I'm feeling like I want to settle down, create a place to live and have a family. Can you beat that?"

"Goodness Matt. I would never have believed it if I hadn't heard it from your own lips. Well now, tell me, what are you doing back here in Wild River?"

"I received a telegram from Sheriff Baxter a couple of months ago. He said that his health is not doing so good and he's looking to find someone to take over his office here. I've thought long and hard about it. I had been working over in New Mexico, and really liked my job. Then, I suddenly got to thinking about this place and what it had meant to me while I was growing up. Finally it got the better of me, and I accepted the job. I guess that I'll start at the first of the month. Now that I have met this pretty lady here, I can't say that I am sorry to be here. Just for the records, Sierra, I clean up real good don't I Molly?"

"You sure do you handsome dog you. Listen, if you like I'll put you up here for tonight and in a couple of days you can find a permanent spot to live. In case I haven't mentioned it Matt, welcome home!"

I returned to the quiet of my own room finding the events of the evening filling my head. Even the event of the day seemed paled against the evening. As I prepared for my bed I kept seeing the sparkle in Matt's eyes as he talked about his life and what he hopes to gain. Yes – everyone has to have some goal in life. Matt may see his come true soon, and God willing, so may I. I must write a letter to Annie and let her know that I love her and maybe, soon, we can be together.

Chapter 5

"My god Sierra, did you just see a ghost?"

"What?"

"Come on girl. What's going on? Your face just drained every ounce of blood from it. Two seconds ago you were laughing and having a great time and now suddenly…"

"Oh, I'm sorry Molly. Must have been something I ate at the luncheon. I seemed to have developed a bad feeling in my stomach. I think I'd better go home and lie down a while. You will excuse me won't you?"

"But you will be at the dance tonight right?"

"I'm sure I'll be fine by then. I really am so sorry."

"Well, if you're sick, you're sick. Just take it easy for a couple of hours. I'm really counting on you to be there tonight."

Trying to smile, I made my exit from the regal celebration being given in the honor of retiring sheriff Clayton Baxter. The few yards to my own place seemed like miles as I pushed my way passed all the celebrants. Everyone seemed to be smiling. Don't suppose the free beer had anything to do with it.

The day had started with a parade down the main street of Wild River Junction. There were even a couple of musicians taking part in it. That is if you could call them musicians. A cart had been hitched to Molly's horse and the piano from the saloon was pushed up into the cart. A gut bucket was picked with great flair and an old miner playing a banjo that looked as if it had been around since the civil war. None the less, it was a grand sight to behold. Then all the local merchants, dressed in their finery marched behind the music wagon. Just their way of saying thanks to Sheriff Baxter for all that he had done for them in the past 23 years. Even though I was the newest merchant in the group, I was very proud that they had included me. Behind the merchants came a long string of residents, in full array, sporting their Sunday finest garments. I would have bet that there wasn't one person who lived in Wild River that didn't participate and give a beaming salute as they passed by the stand that had been erected outside the general store. The stand had been built so that Sheriff Baxter could be up high enough for him to view the stream of friends and well wishers. Molly's friend, Matt, the mayor, his wife and Doc Heller sat beside Sheriff Baxter. I couldn't help but feel a little sad. Here was a man that had given his life to keeping law and order and now there was a war going on inside his body that was causing him to give up his way of life. Losing this war meant losing his life. The rousing send off pulled onto a higher plain when the parade reached the saloon. Molly and her crew had pulled tables and chairs into the street and each table was laded down with delicious looking food. A couple of barrels of beer were being worked with fervor. A sign read, "Free beer. (Until these two barrels are gone.)" On the opposite side of the street there were several more tables laid out with luscious foods. Meats, vegetables and desserts. These tables had been erected by the 'other' town residents. There was an invisible barrier between each side of the road, but they had a common thread. Sheriff Clayton Baxter.

As the eating and the drinking started, Sheriff Baxter and his group joined in the celebration. Sheriff Baxter was called on to say a word to the people. He began by stating that he was absolutely amazed at the number of people that had come to help him celebrate his retirement.

"I've been in Wild River Junction for 24 years. Not until this moment did I realize how many people lived here. In all that time I've been treated with respect and kindness. It was easy for me to do my job. Every one of you knew what it took to make a town a place to be proud of to live in and a safe place to raise our children. Oh, I'm not saying that we're all angels. We know different don't we Mac? Like the time that you thought that a band of bank robbers were coming into town and you had me hide out in the barn with that stinky old mule of yours. I spent the better part of two days inside there. I reckon the temperature had to have been 110 in the shade. Why you wouldn't come and let me know that you had made a mistake, I'll never know. I swear I still smell of that mule. Anyway, it is with much regret that I am retiring from this job. Of course it seems like I don't have much choice. Old Doc here has laid down the law to me. Guess the good Lord deems it necessary for me to step down and give my job to a younger man. I expect every one of you to treat my replacement with as much deference as you awarded me over the years. Remember now, he is a young 'un. But he has had experience with this type of a job. And from what I keep being told, he is very good at it. He comes very highly recommended. Now, before I introduce your new Sheriff let me say 'Thanks'! For all your concerns and the hard work it must have been to get everyone here all gussied up and arriving on time for that great parade. Now, it is my pleasure to introduce you to your new Sheriff. He may not look familiar to all of you, but he is one of our own. He has been gone for a long time, but thank goodness he decided to come home again. Please welcome Sheriff Matthew Rathburn."

It had been at this moment that my blood stopped cold. Matthew Rathburn! That was the name in my family's bible. Why did I not suspect it when Molly introduced me to him? My legs felt as if they couldn't hold me up. I had to leave. Get home and think about it.

Pushing and shoving through the crowds I was finally able to reach the front door of 'Sierra's Finery'. Walking into the darkened interior I made my way to my quarters.

"I have to lie down. I have to think about this." My heart was pounding so hard that I couldn't breathe. Why was it bothering me so much? At last I can find out who he really is and what he had to do with my parents. And what happened to my family? Maybe that was my problem. I wanted to know so much what had happened, and yet I am so afraid to find out what happened.

"Sierra, you don't make any sense. This is your big break to solve the mystery. Pull yourself together. If you didn't want to know the answers, why did you come searching for them? You asked the questions. Now deal with the knowledge that you are about to find out."

I finally realized that I had spoken out loud to myself, and it was then that I knew I had made my decision.

Turning on the lamp to evade the twilight of the late afternoon I looked at myself in the mirror. Hair, a little out of place must have been all that jostling from the crowds. I can fix that. Maybe a different dress would help. No. Perhaps a little color in my cheeks? That would work. I could put a little rouge on my lips too. I promised Molly that I would be there tonight, and I will be. I have another goal to guide me. Matthew Rathburn. You won't know what hit you. Or should I say, who?

Chapter 6

The party was in full swing when Sierra returned to Molly's place. Half the town people were inside and the other half were outside. This was a celebration the likes of which these people had never seen. For the first time in the history of Wild River Junction everyone was willing to put aside any difference's and make the Sheriff's retirement party a rousing success. I noticed Helen Whitt, the mayor's wife, dancing with one of the bartenders from the saloon. Both seemed to be in sync with each other as their feet pranced around the area allotted for a dance floor. Molly had said that Helen was a good old girl. I could see why now. She was having the time of her life. Her husband was watching from across the room, but was more interested in the conversation he was having with the banker than what Helen was doing. Evidently the barrels of beer were still flowing.

"Hey, Sierra! How are you feeling? I was getting ready to send our new Sheriff out to find you."

Molly met me with a broad grin on her face. "Come over here and enjoy some of this wonderful food. One thing about this town, whenever you need the womenfolk to contribute food to a celebration they always bring out the best they can offer. Sit down here and I'll fix you a plate."

"Thanks Molly, but don't make it too much. I'm still a little shaky. Maybe a little glass of milk would help, if you have any."

"Milk! That's no way to celebrate. Can't I talk you into a glass of wine? Hey Matt, come over here and visit with Sierra while I get some fixings." Sierra wanted to object, but it was too late. Matt Rathburn was standing beside her.

"Mind if I sit with you Mrs. Martin? This noisy affair seems to have gotten the best of me. I'm not a rowdy type of man. Things like this I can take, but only in small doses and this one has gone on for too long as far as I'm concerned."

"Please, join me. Tell me Sheriff, what is it that a man like you enjoys to do?"

"Ordinary things I guess. Like being a Sheriff, working with a good hunting dog. Taking a piece of land and making it into something to be proud of. I guess that this kind of get together is necessary once in a while, but I would prefer to be someplace else doing something worthwhile."

"How did you come to accept this position in Wild River Junction?"

"Oh, I was working with a friend as a deputy Sheriff. His town was over run at times with drovers. The main pens for the shipment of cattle were close by, and there were always cattle drives arriving. I guess they thought they were entitled to raise hell after spending months on the trail. Between the two of us we were able to bring about laws that made it easier for him to keep law and order. Pretty soon, we got a reputation of being a 'no nonsense' town. He got everything in hand and I knew that I was no longer needed. I found out about Sheriff Baxter's retirement announcement in one of the bulletins that come every month and that's when I decided to wire him about the job."

"It must be very satisfying to have built a reputation that would allow you to be hired, sight un-seen."

"Well, yes. Of course you know he didn't have much choice, seeing as he needed to be gone as soon as possible. But I fully intend to keep up his good work. He is a terrific man. Fate has dealt him a bad hand."

"Fate has a way of doing that."

"My goodness! So cynical at your early age. Now, tell me how you came about being here in Wild River?"

"Not much to tell really. I worked for a woman in the east. I found her a genius when it came to business. I made up my mind to learn as much as I could and save my money. When I felt I had saved enough I traveled here, opened the shop of my dreams, and here I am."

"You make it sound so easy. But where were you born?"

"Well, I…"

… it was Molly's arrival at the table that made it easy for me to pass over that question. She was laden down with all kinds of goodies. The tray she carried couldn't hold anymore. As she began setting them on the table, I realized that I was hungry. A nice big glass of milk started the feast. I insisted that Matt help me with all that Molly had brought. Between the two of us we managed to make a dent in the feast. The last item, one of Molly's apple pies, disappeared in quick time. Seems that one of Matt's specialties was devouring apple pies.

Feeling over stuffed I stated that I needed to go for a walk to help pack down some of the food that I had ingested. Some good night air seemed to be the required things. As I was leaving the saloon, Matt stepped in beside me and asked if he could accompany me.

"I would be happy for you to."

We walked through the crowds still celebrating in the street and came to my shop. I wanted to go in and seek the seclusion in my quarters, but I suggested that we continue on down the main street. The evening air was still and slightly crisp. Just a part of the moon shone on our heads and million of stars twinkled from far away.

"Sierra, I have really enjoyed visiting with you today. Would you think me bold if I asked if I could see you again?"

"Well, no Matt. I've enjoyed today too, but you must remember, that I am a working girl and I have my business to take care of. Maybe sometime one Sunday. That's when my shop is closed. But then, perhaps you must work on Sundays."

"I am getting a new deputy coming in next Tuesday. He should be able to handle things on a Sunday if I took it off. I don't usually take time off, but I am hoping to start putting my family home back into shape. One day I plan on moving out there and rebuilding the farm. Of course that could be a long way off. Who knows, maybe someday I'll have a wife and family."

"Your family farm Matt? Where is your family farm?"

"It's about five miles from here. No one has been there since I left twelve years ago. I imagine it must be in shambles by now."

"That's sad. Do your parents still live there?"

"No. They don't."

"Where are they then?"

"They… holy molly Clayton! What are you yelling about?"

"Matt, get over here. We got us some boys that think a good fight is a great way to end tonight. I can't handle them by myself."

"Sorry Sierra, I have to go. We'll talk soon."

He scurried off down the street leaving me with a million questions on my lips. He said we would talk soon. How right he was. I couldn't wait to hear his story.

As I prepared myself for bed that night I found myself thinking about Matthew Rathburn. Now that I was over the initial shock of hearing his name I could think with a clearer head. He seemed to be the nice person that Molly had said he was. He certainly was handsome in a tall rugged sort of way. Nothing at all what I had thought him to be that first night that I met him. Maybe he has a good explanation as to how he could possibly be related to me. I guess I'll have to wait and see. Amid the buzzing of the existing crowd outside, I fell asleep and dreamt of my parents and Matt.

Chapter 7

'Sierra's Finery' kept me busy all week. I couldn't believe how many women came in and purchased my lovely things. I had never dreamed that it would be such a success. In my wildest dreams I had visions of having two maybe three customers a day, but never did I dream that I could reach out to so many. There were even some ladies that came on the coach from the next town. It seems that the reputation of the quality of my goods had traveled like wildfire. I knew that I would have to order two of everything from now on.

I saw Matt from time to time from the inside of my shop. He would be walking through the streets and on one occasion he was accompanied by a lovely young lady that I recognized as being the daughter of the Mayor and Helen. I presumed that the young man I saw with him on more than one occasion was the deputy he had told me about. He was a gangly young man. Sandy colored hair, very tall. He was almost a head taller than Matt. I tried to guess what his name should be, but nothing I thought of seemed to fit him. A couple of days later I was opening up my door as he was passing by. He stopped, raised his hat and introduced himself.

"Howdy mam'. My name is Jethro Lepowitz. I'm the new deputy sheriff here in town. I just thought I would introduce myself to you. If there is anything that I can do for you, please let me know."

"I'm very pleased to meet you Jethro. My name is Sierra Martin. The Sheriff told me he was getting a new deputy. He didn't tell me you would be so handsome though. Thank you for your kindness."

"Good day mam'."

And with this he replaced his hat on his head and strode off down the street. His legs were so long that he seemed to cover the distance from my shop to the Sheriff's office in no time at all.

Sunday in town was a special day. The small church was surrounded with horses and buggies and seemed to be a place, not only for worship, but for fellowship too. Many of the families would holler greetings to each other and invite them to their place for a fine Sunday lunch. I had not been into the church since coming here. I don't know why. Guess that I told myself that I was just too busy. But maybe, I didn't want to admit that I had lost my faith. I seemed to flounder around with the teachings of my parents against the teachings of life. Life had not been good to me; therefore it was God's fault. How can God be so cruel to a person and make them live the life that I had had to endure. But then maybe I had not been what God wanted me to be. Was I that bad?

On this Sunday, as I listened to the church bells ringing and saw all the people of the congregation happily entering the church, I felt a pull. Maybe if I went in for this one Sunday I could fathom out my feelings. I can always leave early. (You know you won't). So, I pulled on my bonnet and swung the knitted stole around my shoulders and went through my shop door.

Only a few steps down the wooden sidewalk, then off onto the dirt road and shortly at the foot of the steps leading up into the church. Hesitating, I took a deep breath. Then suddenly I found an arm around my waist and I was being propelled up the steps and into the church. Recovering, immediately I turned and saw that my helper was none other than Sheriff Matthew Rathburn himself.

"Just what do you think your doing Matt?"

"Well you looked as if you might have a hard time climbing up the stairs so I thought I would help you."

"You scared me half to death."

"I'm sorry. You were meaning to come into church weren't you?"

"Yes, but in my own way."

"Well next time I'll just walk right past you. I didn't mean to upset you."

"That's alright. I just wasn't prepared for it is all."

"Hey, before the reverend gets started I want to ask you if you would like to spend some time with me today?"

"Oh! I – well, can I let you know after services?"

"Sure you can. But don't take too long to answer. I'm planning on going out to my old homestead right after services. I want to see what I need to do to make it a fit place to live. Of course, if you would rather not go out there with me I'll understand."

"Oh! Actually, I would love to go with you. Pick me up in a half an hour after services. That will give me time to change into something a little less frilly."

"Bringing in the sheaves. Bringing in the sheaves. We shall come rejoicing. Bringing in the sheaves." This was the song that began the service. All there sang with much gusto and emphasis. I felt strangely moved. I somehow knew that all my fellow townspeople had a connection with God through this song. Can I change my feelings? Who knows? I only know that I am excited about going with Matt out to the ranch. Maybe now I can get my answers. But I can't tell him my story. Not yet. I have many bridges to cross before I can do that.

The service seemed to take forever. The reverend spent so much time informing us all about the devil and the evil that people do and how we must not listen to the devil. We must shout out and make him leave us alone least we forfeit our souls. His exuberance kept many a parishioner from falling asleep. Finally, the ending prayer and then the singing of the song that lead us cheerfully out of the church. I shook hands with the reverend, told him that his sermon was very interesting and made my escape.

I had barely buttoned up the pair of riding breeches that I was wearing before I heard the sound of a horse and buggy pull up in front of my shop. I quickly pulled on a shirt and waistcoat, then my boots. A knock at the door told me that Matt was waiting. Tying my hair up behind my head with a blue ribbon, I ran to the door. Matt helped me into the seat of the buggy and with a quick tug on the reins, we were off.

With the deep blue of the sky up above us, the big white puffy clouds made such a contrast. Around us lay the eternal land of grasses and red clay dirt. We passed by Mrs. MacAffee's boarding house and in a northerly direction we left the town behind. At first the trail was easy to see, but then about 2 miles out of town we turned west. Here the trail was barely visible to the naked eye. Just a few pleasantries had passed between Matt and I since we began our ride.

"This trail doesn't seem to have been used in years."I remarked to Matt.

"I know. When I lived out here it was well traveled and marked by the constant use of horses and wagons that used to come out here. I doubt that anyone has been out here since I left. I've wanted to come ever since I came into town, but I've been so busy getting everything set at the Sheriff's office. Hey I heard that you met my side kick Jethro. What do you think of him? He's kind' a green behind the ears, but he has all the makings of a good deputy."

"Yes, he introduced himself the other day. He seemed to be a very polite young man."

"He thinks your something special. To quote him 'She is so beautiful and you can tell she is a real lady'.""

"Well! I hope I don't disappoint him in any way. Tell me Matt, why did you leave your home here?'

"It's a long story. Sometime I'll tell you, but right now we are coming up on the gate to the property. See that sign on the left? I helped my dad carve that. We decided that our place was so special that we needed to have a name for it. I remember, one night we sat at the supper table and the three of us put our heads together to come up with a name. Mom wanted something romantic, like Camelot. Pop said we would have all the neighbors laughing at that one. I wanted to name it Rocking Chair Ridge. This would let everyone know that the old rocker on the porch had rocked a ridge into the wood. But pop only laughed and said no way. Finally, pop looked over at mom and said, 'how about the 'Welcome Home Again Ranch'. I saw right away what that meant to mom, and so, that's what we called this ranch. Welcome Home Again."

"I don't understand Matt. Why was that name so mean-ingful to them?"

We were pulling up inside the yard area before Matt spoke again.

"Here Sierra, let me help you down. Now be careful where you step. Never know what might be hiding in this tall grass."

Carefully we made our way to the door. The porch slats were splintered and rotting. As we walked through the doorway, we found it hanging off its hinges. Matt stopped and looked around the room. Nothing but dirt, dust and cobwebs could be seen. Foot prints were in the dust on the floor.

"Someone's been in here. Not too long ago either. Oh well, there isn't anything here that anyone would want. But I wonder why someone would come here. It looks to me like it was a woman."

"Why on earth would you come to that conclusion?"

"Well, just look. Small petite footprints then every once in a while the floor looks as if it had been touched by the swooshing movement of a long skirt. See the way the dust has been disturbed."

"Wow! You're good! I bet you're a terrific hunter. No wonder you are a sheriff. I bet you can track any human or animal."

"Well, I had a good teacher. Pop was the best. We never went hungry. But he only hunted for food, not for the sport of it."

"Matt, where are your parents now?"

"They're dead".

"Oh, I'm so sorry. What happened?"

Matt walked over to the old chair in the kitchen by the fire and ran his hands lovingly over it.

"Mom used to spend hours in this kitchen. She would cook all day and then at night she would sit in this chair doing her mending or darning. She could repair a hole in a sock so that no one else would ever guess that it had been there. She would also make sure that I did my homework. They were both bound and determined that I was going to excel in my studies. They had big plans for my future."

"Matt! What happened?"

"When I was ten years old my real mom died. She was the only soul that I had in this world. My real father had mysteriously disappeared when mom found out she was pregnant. I suspect that they weren't married. Anyway, I was shuffled from orphanage to orphanage. When I was thirteen I ran away from home 'to seek my fortune.' I had read all kinds of books in the orphanages about being someone special and I wanted to prove to the world that I was someone. Not just some kid that had no one and had to rely on the church for his home and food. I managed to last on my own for about two years. I traveled all over the country, mostly on foot, or on the back of some drovers mount. When I arrived here in Wild River I was pretty travel worn and sick to death of it. I managed to make a couple of dollars a month by doing odd jobs. One day this wagon came into town and it was full of boxes of vegetables. I followed it to the general store and as the man driving the wagon jumped to the ground I offered to help him unload his wagon for the price of a meal. I remember he looked at me for a long time. He had a very quizzical look in his eyes.

"Can you do a good job lad?" he had asked.

"Yes sir. If I don't you don't have to pay me." I had replied.

"Well, let's see what you've got. I'll be inside the store. Take each of these crates off of the wagon and take them around to the back door. I'll meet you there.'

I did exactly as he had asked and when my chore was finished I found myself inside the local saloon sitting at a table on which there was the biggest steak I have ever seen sizzling on a platter. The big potato setting next to it just sizzled and was coated with butter. For dessert I ate half an apple pie. I'll never forget that meal. I had never eaten like that in my whole entire life. All the while I was eating Mr. Rathburn, that was his name, was asking questions about where I was heading, how long did I think I going to be in Wild River, what kind of schooling had I had.

Before the evening was over, I was sitting on that wagon seated next to Mr. Rathburn. We were heading out into the night, heading for his ranch. He told me that he and his wife had a small farm. They had a few heads of stock, but they also had a lot of chickens and that Mrs. Rathburn grew all kinds of vegetables. They made their money by selling the eggs, chickens, and vegetables to the general store and the eating place in the saloon. They would never be rich, but they sure were happy in their little world. They had hopes that some day they could clear some of their acreage and grow some crops.

That was when it all began for me. They took me into their home and treated me as if I was a son. I found so much happiness with them. We all worked hard on the farm and it started to pay off. I had found my family and it pleased them that I called them mom and pop.

One day pop said that it was time for us to be a real family. He took me and mom into town and we spoke to a lawyer. They told the lawyer that they wanted to adopt me and give me their name. Well, within a short time I was standing in front of a judge and he asked me if I was sure that I wanted the Rathburns to adopt me. I quickly answered yes and he then stated that I was now Matthew Barnes Rathburn. Just that easy! That night we celebrated. At last! I was someone. When we got home that night, pop climbed into the attic and brought down the family bible. On the front page he entered my name under the page heading : SON. It was official."

Matt paused, lost in the memory of his story. Then he told me to wait. He crossed the room and climbed up the stairs that lead to the loft. I could hear him moving around up there, muttering away to himself. He then backed his way down the stairs. "Darn! Someone's stolen the Bible. It was always kept up there on the special table under the window."

I couldn't bring myself to tell him that the bible was safe in my room. At last I had found out why his name was in it. How like my parents to take someone into their hearts. But had they forgotten me by then? Did they think of me once in a while? Did they think I was dead? And I still haven't found out what happened to them.

Chapter 8

We spent several hours at the farm. Matt was astounded that it had deteriorated so badly. The barn would have to be taken down totally and a new one put up in its place. There were only two walls standing and one of them was leaning badly. The roof had fallen into the center of the walls and he could tell that there would be nothing that could be salvaged.

"It must have been that bad storm that came through here five years ago. I had heard that it nearly annihilated Wild River Junction. Old man Johnson and his wife who lived just a couple of miles from here were picked up and carried several hundred feet by the twister before they fell back to earth. It killed them both. I guess I thought that this place would last forever."

The fences around the land were in bad shape too. Some were standing, others leaning over or missing altogether. They looked like the teeth of an old miner. The barbed wire had coiled itself into a knot. It set there waiting for us to try to move it. It almost dared us. The rust and the barbs made it all look so sinister. The chicken coups were gone and so was the pen for the horses. I could still see the farm the way it was when I had lived here.

"You know Sierra, this can be a great place again. Looking around I see that it needs a lot of work, but it's nothing that I can't do with a little help. I bet I could get someone from town to help me when I'm out here."

"But Matt, would you have the time? I mean now that you're Sheriff and all. This work will take a couple of years to complete if you can only work on it one day a week. I mean really, be sensible. Maybe you should sell the land and let someone else do the work."

"Sell this farm! Are you crazy? This land is the only tangible thing that I have in this world. I could have sold it before I left here twelve years ago but I wouldn't. I knew that some day I would be back and when I am through being Sheriff I will make my living on this land."

"Sorry Matt. I didn't understand."

"Well, are you ready to go back into town? I want to get there before dark and check up on Jethro. This is the first time he's been all alone protecting the townspeople. I want to make sure it isn't the townspeople having to protect him."

"Matt, before we go, tell me, what happened to your folks."

"Well they had had a daughter once. This was before I came into the picture. One morning mom got up and was fixing breakfast for the three of them. There was a knock on the door. Pop thought that maybe it was old Doc stopping by on his way back into town, but it wasn't. It was someone they had never seen before. He told pop that he hadn't eaten for several days and he was willing to do any chore if they would only feed him. Well, mom, having the heart of an angel told him to sit down and eat breakfast with them and then they would discuss his earning it. He made a good impression on mom and pop and he stuck around for several days doing odd jobs and helping pop with some of the heavy work. He seemed real taken with their daughter and she with him. She was about five years old. One day Pop asked him if he would take the wagon into town and pick up a special delivery that was coming in on the freight wagon. He was pleased that Pop would trust him with this delivery, and before he left he suggested that he take the girl with him.

Pop's last words he said to him as he pulled out was, "Don't forget to bring her home with you."

It was many hours later that Pop began to get a cold feeling up his spine. The twilight of evening was coming over the hills. Darkness would follow quickly. It shouldn't have taken them more than a couple of hours to make the round trip. Maybe there had been an accident on the trail. Maybe the freight wagon had got in late and they had to wait for it. No! Old Henry is always within a half an hour of his schedule. You can almost set your clock by him. Figured he had better saddle up the mare and go and find them. He told mom that he would come back in about two hours and they would be with him. When he got into town he went directly to the freight office. The old freight wagon was there, but Henry had already quit for the day. Pop found him in the saloon. It seems that Henry had never seen either one of them. Neither the helper nor his daughter. Checking further Pop couldn't find anyone that had seen them there that day. Pop went to the Sheriff's Office and talked to Sheriff Baxter. He explained everything to him and told him how worried he was. Sheriff Baxter said that because it was dark out now he would get a couple of guys together in the morning and ride out to the farm and see if there were any signs as to what direction the wagon went. It broke Pops heart to have to ride home and tell Mom that they were no where to be found. The next morning the group of townsfolk came out and began the search. They found that just a half mile from the farm, the wagon had turned off the trail and headed east across the plain. The tracks were very obvious and it was easy going. They had followed the ruts for about five miles when they saw the wagon up ahead. Spurring their horses on they quickly covered the ground. The wagon was empty. Pop called out to his daughter again and again, hoping that maybe they were walking close by. Nothing! Why would they come this way and then leave the wagon? Sheriff Baxter was the first to realize what happened. One half of a mile from the wagon they found railroad tracks. He figured that they must have flagged down the train as it slowed for a water stop. That train would be miles away by now. They raced back to town and talked to the station master. They found out that the train would have stopped there around noon the day before and it was heading east. There would be many stops before it got to its destination and many people getting on and getting off. It would be almost impossible to know where they were. Pop spent many weeks traveling on that same train getting on and off asking if anyone had seen a man with a little girl. No one could help him. Sheriff Baxter wired the information to towns across the easterly direction hoping that someone would see them. It was to no avail. Finally they gave up their search. Mom was totally broken hearted. Pop told me that it wasn't until I came into their lives that she began to live again.

Well, one day about twelve years ago, an old miner was in the saloon and was telling about a man that he had panned gold with up in the hills of California. He had told this miner that he had visited Wild River Junction and that it was a great place to live and then when he struck it rich he would be heading back. It seems that this buddy had with him a young girl. He claimed that it was his wife, but she sure didn't act that way. He pretty much kept her locked up. When word got to Mom and Pop, they jumped into their wagon and raced into town to speak to this miner. The weather was pretty bad that day and Pop had asked me to bring in the couple of horses that had wandered of in the night. I was just returning when they passed me on the trail. I had never seen Pop drive his team that hard and they were flying. I had corralled the horses and walked into the house. It had been cold outside and I warmed myself in front of the fire. Wondering if there was anything to eat on the stove, I found a note from mom. 'We may have news about our daughter. We have gone to talk to man in town.'

It was a couple of hours later that I heard a single rider come up to the front of the house. I opened the door and found Sheriff Baxter there. He looked grim and I knew that something was wrong. He told me that Mom and Pop's wagon had overturned on the last curve on the trail. Both of them were badly hurt and that Doc was with them. I saddled my horse and rode beside Sheriff Baxter into town. I hardly waited for my horse to stop before I was off. I ran up the stairs to Doc's office. He met me at the door. I'll never forget it. He told me that their injuries were just too severe. They had both died.

Chapter 9

The ghost of things past showed on the face of the man I was facing. Unashamedly the tears ran down his face. I think that my heart stopped for that moment. Both of us were suffering with the knowledge that the two most wonderful people in the world had died because of me, their daughter. They were hurrying to town to find someone who might be able to answer the question of what had happened to me. I could also understand just how important they had been in Matt's life. We both stood there, not looking at each other but off into that vast unknown area of sorrow. Matt's eyes seemed dazed and I knew that I could not tell him that I was that little girl from so long ago.

"Sorry Sierra. I haven't talked about what happened for a long time. I just couldn't bring myself to face the truth. It happened so quickly. Pop had often talked about clearing an area just over the rise out back and building a nice white picket fence around it. He thought it would be a perfect place for him and mom to spend eternity. I remember I spent that night out there preparing the ground for them. After the funeral, I built the white picket fence just the way they wanted it. It was the last thing that I did here before I left. I felt that without them I couldn't stay here. After all, it wasn't my property. It belonged to that little girl. Maybe one day she would return and claim it. I didn't know that Pop had told Doc before he died that I was to have the land. It was several years later that I found this out. Sheriff Baxter had been talking to a man that I was working with down in Arizona. Sheriff sent me a note telling me to come back and take care of my property. I was astounded. But I just couldn't bring myself to come back. I sure am glad that I finally did though. It wasn't fair to Pop my staying away. He had put his heart and soul into this land, and here I let it go back to weeds and ruin. But I'm going to make up for it now. I really want this."

"I'm happy for you Matt. Sometime we leave the path that God has designated for us. We do it because of the effect others have on our lives. Most times we can't control it. It's only when we finally reach that point where we can truthfully say, this is my life. Now I will make it what I want it to be."

"Sounds like you've had some hard knocks yourself Sierra. Someday you'll have to tell me all about your life."

"Maybe. Some day, but not right away. I'm still trying to get my life right."

We walked side by side down the steps to the path. It suddenly seemed such a natural thing to do, to walk beside this man. The horse was grazing on the tall grass that surrounded the area and didn't look too happy when we climbed into the buggy. Matt shook the reins and made a clicking sound. The animal looked around at us as if to say hey I was content as it was. We both burst out laughing as the buggy started to move. Some of the tension that had been between Matt and I seemed to have eased. I had seen a side of him that few had probably seen. He was a caring, loving and appreciative person. My heart really ached for him and the loss he had suffered. But then, what of my loss? I had lost Mom and Pop years ago myself. But then, I was only a small child. I had had to adapt to a new way of life. Matt had been almost a grown-up when the tragedy struck.

We talked of many little things on the ride back to town. How great the weather had been since I came here. What a great friend Molly was to both of us. Matt told me stories about Molly that made me laugh. Something I hadn't done in a long time. It felt so good. Matt also told me that Doc had been a real friend to him when he was first in Wild River Junction. It was really because of Doc that he had decided to work odd jobs in town. It had been hard. He had been just a young kid trying to make a couple of dollars so that he could survive. He said that he used to live in a shed out back of Doc's office. Once in a while he would sweep the steps in front of Doc's office and then the porch. Doc wanted to pay him, but he felt he needed to do something to repay Doc for letting him stay under a roof.

Matt had found this old bed laying out in a field one day. Doc talked the freight manager into loaning Matt his wagon. Matt went out, picked up this rusty old bed and brought it back to Doc's. He spent a whole week washing and brushing the dirt and rust from the bed. Finally he put it into his shed. It took up most of the room, but he was so proud of it. Doc surprised him with an old mattress filled with hay. They both were excited that at last Matt would have a good place to sleep. Matt decided that he would try it out while Doc was there. He smilingly jumped into the center of the mattress and Crr-Bang. The bed collapsed onto the floor. They finally figured out that the bed had rusted through and just wouldn't hold the weight. At first Matt had been angry after all he had put a lot of time and effort into it. But then Doc started to laugh. He said that he had never seen anyone with such a surprised look on their face. It was the funniest thing Doc had every seen. Finally Matt could see the funny side of this calamity, and they both laughed until their sides hurt. Matt said that Doc had tears running down his face. They finally decided to take the bed out and just leave the mattress on the floor. That way, Doc said, Matt couldn't fall any further.

As we neared town, Matt slowed the pace of the buggy. He seemed to be deep in thought.

"Sierra, thanks for coming with me today. I really had a great time. I know that I got a little maudlin, telling you about Mom and Pop, but thanks for putting up with me. I really have a good feeling about that place now. I am so anxious to get started with repairs. Wow! Repairs! I probably should say the re-building. Would you like to come out some

Sunday and see what we can get into? I don't mean that I want you to do any work, but just be there to cheer me on."

"Matt I would love to cheer you on. Please let me know when you're going to go out there and maybe I can help re-do the furniture. It looked to me that it wasn't so bad. A new coat of stain would work wonders."

"Thanks, Sierra."

"Matt, you can stop by my shop and let me out. I have a couple of chores to finish before I go to bed and tomorrow being Monday I want to be sure that my shop is ready for anything. I have been so pleased about the way the women of Wild River have accepted me and my goods. Things have gone so much better than I would every have hoped for. I had no idea that there were so many outlying ranches and farms in this area. But good for me, in each of those ranches and farms are women."

"I'm very happy for you Sierra. I hope that it means you will be around here for a while. I would hate to see you leave. We have all become accustomed to seeing your smiling face. And a beautiful one at that I might say."

"Matt Rathburn, you must be part Irish to come up with blarney like that."

"Don't know, Sierra. I never have been able to find out what I could be 'part' of. "

Reaching my shop, Matt pulled the buggy to a stop and jumped down. He came around to my side and reached up with his hands to help me down. His fingers circled around my waist and I could swear that I felt a shock pass through my body. It seemed like slow motion as he brought me down to the sidewalk. I wanted his hands to stay around me. I didn't want him to let me go. I think I gasped a little. What was wrong with me? I can't feel this way. I can't afford to feel this way about anyone. I have my plans to finish. Maybe, after I have my life settled I can think about it, but not now.

"Sierra, can we maybe have supper together some night this week?"

"Well Matt, I'm not sure just what I am going to be into for the next couple of days. Why don't we just wait and see what this week brings for both of us. But thank you for a lovely day."

Matt waited until I was inside my shop before he climbed back into the buggy and led the horse off. I felt that I had disappointed him in some way. I don't want to lose him as a friend, but the way I'm beginning to feel I must keep this relationship to a minimum.

I wondered if I would ever tell him about my life story. I doubt it. I don't know of any reason that I would need to do that.

Lighting the lamp in my quarters I looked around me. I was so close to my dream. All those shadows that have been hiding my dreams will be illuminated and very soon I can bring everything out into the open. How will that feel, I wondered. I have been so up tight and scared for so long I just can't imagine life without this heaviness on my shoulders. Just a few more months, and it will all be done.

I wondered if Matt would be willing to be just friends for a while. The idea of he and I being more caused me to hold my breath. This is so silly. I hardly know the man, and yet, after today, I feel that I want to know more about him. I wonder if he's thinking about me tonight? Did I just imagine the spark between us? Being true to myself, I answered yes. Do I really want it that way? Yes. But being the sensible person that I have to be I know that I must keep him at arms length.

Pulling my night gown down over my head I felt a slight tremor go through my body. I was remembering how it had felt when Matt had his hands around my waist. Quickly, I doused the light and climbed into bed. Thank you God for such a great day and please, help me to focus on what I must do, I prayed.

Chapter 10

Matt made it easy for me for the following couple of weeks. We would meet on the street and casually acknowledged each other. I felt bad to be so cool. But my mind was made up. I have to admit though, each time I saw him I would feel a little tug on my heart strings. Then one day when I was writing up a purchase for a customer, I heard the tinkling of my door bell and when I looked up, there he was in all his glory.

"Why, Sheriff! I never thought I'd see you in this shop." My customer stated exactly what I was thinking.

"Hello Mrs. Davis. I have some business that I need some help with. I'm sure that Mrs. Martin would be the perfect person to do that. By the way Mrs. Davis, how are the twins doing? I heard that they came home from boarding school the other day. I hope that everything's alright?"

"Well thank you for asking Sheriff. But there's nothing wrong. They have both been doing so well in school that Mr. Davis and I decided to give them a treat and let them come home for a few days."

"Great. Please give Mr. Davis my regards."

"I certainly will. You will probably be seeing him and the boys in a couple of days. We need to order more lumber so that we can build another room onto the house. The boys are getting so big they can hardly both fit into the small bedroom they have now. Well, I thank you Mrs. Martin. You have been very helpful as usual. I'm anxious to show Mr. Davis my new dress. See you very soon."

"Bye Mrs. Davis and thank you for coming by." As Mrs. Davis left the shop Matt walked gingerly over to the counter.

"So! This is where you spend your days. It's a very cozy room. I must admit that I had to think twice before I talked myself into deciding to actually come inside here. I bet everyone in town will know before the days over. Mrs. Davis will for sure tell anyone she meets about the Sheriff being inside 'Sierra's Finery For Women'.

"I must admit that I too am astonished to see you walking in here. What is this important business that you must discuss with me?"

"Well! Actually, I told a little white lie. I don't have any business to talk about. It was the first thing I thought up to explain to Mrs. Davis as to why I was here."

"Wow! The mystery deepens. Is it maybe that you need to buy a new nightgown for your first night at the farm. Or maybe a new nightcap! Am I getting close?"

"No! Not anywhere near to being close. Please don't let anyone hear you say those things. I'd be the laughing stock of the town."

"Well, if it's not that, what is it?"

"It has recently come to my attention that each year at this time Wild River Junction celebrates the end of summer with a dance. People all over the county come and there's a group of good musicians that come and play. I know that being a new comer to this area you probably haven't heard about this, so I thought that I would let you know."

"Thank you Matt. But actually I do know about it. I have had several customers come in and order special dresses for this occasion. They are all very excited about it."

"Oh! Well, would you consider going with me to the dance? I know that we haven't exactly been real friendly since our ride out to the farm, but I promise that I won't talk about anything that would be boring or sad. I figure that's what made you back off from our relationship."

"Oh Matt! No, that wasn't it at all. I just couldn't explain to you how important my plan for the future is. It's very complicated. I really want a relationship with you, but not now. Can you understand that?"

"I'm not sure I understand. But as long as you don't close me out of your life entirely I guess that I will trust you to explain someday in the future."

"Thank you Matt. And I promise that I will explain. But your trusting me for now is very important."

"Alright then. Now, do you want to go to the dance with this old cowboy or not?"

"I would be honored to go with you, as long as you remember the rules of our friendship."

"Damn! Will you put the rules in writing for me? That way I'll be sure to follow them to the letter."

"I am sure that you are too much of a gentleman to need the rules written down."

"I'll try to be. Let's say I pick you up one week from Saturday at 6 p.m. I expect you to be dressed fit to kill looking like a princess. Did I mention that it is a fancy dress dance? No! Well, it is. I have to find my extra fine Sunday go to meeting suit for that night. Hope it still fits. Thanks Sierra. I was afraid that I would have to ask one of Mayor Whitt's daughters. Believe me, there isn't a pretty one in the bunch."

"I know. They've all been in here to order dresses. I'm so happy that I've saved you from that chore. But you will have to dance with them at the affair won't you?"

"Not if I can outrun them. Besides, I'm the kind of an escort that dances only with the one that I brought with me."

"Is that so? Does that mean that I can't dance with anyone else?"

"Well, only if they are under 16 and over 70."

"That doesn't give me much choice."

"That's the idea."

"Thanks Matt for asking me. I'm looking forward to it. One week from Saturday, at 6 p.m. sharp. And I am to look like a princess."

"You always look like a princess. See you around town. Goodbye Sierra."

His eyes lingered for a moment on me then he was gone. It will be all right. It's only one night. Yet why do I feel so bubbly inside? Calm down Sierra. You're acting as if you were 16 years old, but what a great feeling! Maybe this is wrong. I said that I was going to stay away from him for awhile. Why didn't I just say NO? Because I didn't want to that's why. Oh why do I always do battle with myself. Is it because I was born a Pisces the symbol of the two fishes. One fish is trying to swim upstream and the other trying to swim downstream. How true. My life seemed to reflect that in so many ways. Well, the damage is done. I'll go with Matt and everything will be just fine. It will be only what I make of it. Now, what does a princess wear to a formal dance?

* * * *

The soft chiffon outer skirt slide slowly down over my head. I had taken great pains picking out my dress. I wanted to be sure that it was nothing like any that I had sold in the past two weeks. It was blue. But not just any old blue. The color in the fabric shimmered and shone as if there were stars in it. The neckline was as decent as it could be and yet still show the crease between my breasts. I had never thought too much about my breast before, but this dress certainly had me conscious of the fact that Mother Nature had been good to me. My waist may be a little too thick though. All the good food that Molly keeps feeding me has done the damage. But, all in all, when the last curl was in place and a little rouge rubbed into my checks and on my lips I felt that I was a princess. My prince would be calling for me at any minute. I hoped that he would be pleased with the way I looked.

When I answered the knock on the shop door I was taken aback by what I saw. A tall dark handsome man wearing the finest suit I have ever seen. Here was my prince.

"What? Do I look bad?"

"Oh! No! Matt! You look fine. No! You look more than fine."

"I had better look fine. I have to escort the most beautiful women I have ever seen to the dance tonight. Sierra, you look magnificent. You literally take my breath away."

He took my hand and lifted it to his lips. The whisper of a kiss brushed the back of my hand. He glanced up to look into my face. His eyes bore into my heart. I felt that he knew somehow the way I felt about him.

"Well my beautiful princess. Your carriage waits. Allow me to escort you to your seat."

"Thank you my Lord. It will be my pleasure."

With that we were on our way. Who knew what the night ahead held for us. I imagine lots of dancing, eating and laughing. Well, I'd better go light on the eating part.

But fate had something else in mind that night. No pleasures for Sierra. No laughing. Just pure terror!

Chapter 11

Matt pulled the buggy up to the town hall. I've seen excitement in my life, but not to the extent of the faces all around me were such beautiful women and handsome men. All dressed in their finest array. A young man helped me down from the buggy. He waited until Matt came to my side before he jumped into the driver's seat and was gone in a flash, urging our horse to giddy-up. Matt offered his arm to me and I put my hand through it. His other hand closed around my hand and we entered the celebration. The music hadn't started yet. Everyone was waiting in anticipation. Many hellos could be heard, and smiling faces beamed the words. I spotted Molly across the way and we made an attempt to cover the ground between us. She looked fabulous. Wearing a dress that I had never seen before, she absolutely shimmered. Sequins covered her body and her jewelry shone as only a true stone can do. She appeared to be in the company of her Faro dealer. He was dressed in black from head to toe except for the paisley design on his waist-coat. This sparkled in tune with what Molly was wearing. They were a very handsome couple. When Molly realized that we were heading her way, she gathered her escort to her side and waved a greeting to us.

"Matt. Sierra. I'm so glad you could come early. I was having a little trouble saving your seats. Thought I was going to have to punch Harriet Thomas in the snout. She insisted that she should have these chairs. Brad here finally convinced her that she would be so much better off closer to the musicians. Brad can talk anyone into anything. He has a real silver tongue. Matt, you know Brad don't you? And Sierra, I don't know if I have introduced you two before. Brad just came into town two days ago, but I have known him for a lot of years. There was a time when we thought we wanted to get married. But then we sobered up and heaved a big sigh of relief. Brad is going to be in town for a couple of weeks, so I put him to work. I guarantee that I'll make money while he is here. Oh not that he isn't honest. He is just very good at what he does."

"Hello, Brad. It's been a long time since we've seen each other. Sierra, I was just a kid last time I saw Brad. I knew he and Molly were thick and I hated him for it. Molly was my girl. Or at least I pretended she was. Nobody was as happy as I was when he left here. What have you been doing all these years, Brad?"

"Well, I tried my hand on the river boats. You know, they have experienced gamblers on them now. I didn't do too badly. Unfortunately one of the passengers I had gambled with decided to forgo his usual late night toddy. He came back to his cabin early and caught me in bed with his wife. I had to make a mad dash and the only thing that saved me was a sand bar that was close by where I dove into the water. I had to leave all my belongings and money behind. It taught me a lesson though. Always wear a money belt. Even when you're making love!"

"Same old Brad! What happened after that?"

"I spent a couple of nights on the sand bar and then a boat came by and picked me up. I then went to California. Hit a gold mining town called Rough and Ready. It's quite a place. They have a town motto there that states 'Where the men are rough and the women are ready.' You had better believe it. They're a tough bunch of bastards. I kinda roamed around from one mining town to the next for several years. Then I got itching to see some civilized people again.

Worked my way across the country and here I am. Right now I feel that I'll never leave."

"Yea, sure Brad! Where have I heard that before?" Molly was smiling as she spoke.

There was a sparkle in her eyes as she looked at Brad. You could see a definite comfort in the relationship between the two of them.

While Brad had been talking, the musicians were making their way onto the stage. There were six of them. Each had that typical countrified appearance. They began to tune up their instruments and on a cue from their leader, they jumped into a hoe down. The floor literally shook. The rousing rendition brought couples to the dance floor, and soon the flurry of colors twisting and turning and changing were all you could see. Almost like a kaleidoscope, when you twist it and the patterns and colors change. How exciting it was. Matt asked me if I would mind if we sat this one out. He wasn't too up on this hoe down type of dancing. When they played a slow one he would dance. I laughed at his embarrassment of admitting that he couldn't dance. I really didn't mind. It was so much fun to watch the people on the dance floor. One of the young men that worked at the feed store came over and asked me to dance, but I politely thanked him and said no. I was astounded to see Molly and Brad out there. They looked as if they had danced together many times before. Each step was entwined perfectly with the other one. I admired Molly so much. She'd had a hard life, but it hadn't made her bitter at all. She was just a happy go lucky person. She deserved all the fun she could get.

The set finally came to an end and the dancers strolled off the floor. Many women were fanning themselves and I could see the sweat glistening on the foreheads of most of the men. Then, the slow strains of a melody started and Matt was before me with his hand reaching out. I curtsied, and put my hand on his arm. We floated around the dance floor. Not seeing the blur of people on the sidelines. As we danced, we became one. Not caring what people were thinking, we stared into each others eyes and blotted out the whole world. It wasn't until we heard a thunderous applause we realized that the music had stopped but we were still dancing. I laughed a little, but was embarrassed too. Matt just hung his head and led me back to our seats.

"What are you two trying to do, start a rumor?" Molly asked as I sat down.

"Sorry Molly. I don't know what happened. I suddenly went deaf."

"Yeah! Right!"

As the music started up again, Matt asked if I wanted anything to drink and when I replied yes, he went over to the refreshment table and selected a cup of punch. Before he brought it back to me though he visited the keg in the corner and poured himself a glass of beer. With the head foaming over the lip of the glass, he took a big swallow. He glanced up and seemed to have a white mustache on his upper lip. I smiled and his expression was asking 'what's so funny?' By the time he reached me with my punch, I was laughing out loud.

"Well I'm glad that I can amuse you Sierra."

"Oh Matt. It's just that it looks so funny on your lip. Here, take my hanky and wipe it off."

How wonderful to be able to laugh with someone. This moment was very precious to me. I knew that Matt was becoming more to me than just a friend. Right this minute, I didn't mind.

The musicians had decided to take a beer break and they left the stage. The atmosphere in the hall was electrifying. Everyone was enjoying this evening. These occasions don't come too often. When they happen, they are enjoyed to the fullest.

Molly and Brad had decided to take in a breath of fresh air during the break. I suspected that the little silver flask that I saw in Brad's pocket was to be the feature point of their intermission.

Finally, the band was back on the stage. They were asking for requests. It seems that they could play anything. I heard several people shouting out the names of tunes, and then I heard a familiar voice ask, "Can you play 'Let me Call You Sweetheart'?"

I froze in my chair.

"Alright Sierra," I told myself, "Don't be stupid. Lots of people like that song." Suddenly I realized that I was holding my breath. "Now, breathe in and out. Don't let it get to you. Focus on Matt. Everything is fine."

"Sierra, what happened?"

"Oh! I guess that the excitement and the dancing got to me a little. But I'm alright now though."

"I'll get you another glass of punch. When I come back we'll take a walk outside and get you some fresh air. Is that alright?"

"Thank you Matt, you are too kind."

As Matt walked away, the out of body feeling began to fade. How could I have been so upset by that song title? Will I never get over the terror I feel whenever I hear it. Someday I hope.

Deep in thought at that moment I didn't see him until he was standing before me. He was offering his hand to me. He wanted me to dance. I slowly looked up into the face that I knew only too well.

"Well if it isn't my lovely Sierra. How fortunate to meet again. I've looked for you everywhere. I almost gave up, but something kept prodding me to continue my quest.

Now, they're playing our song I believe. Dance with me my love."

"No! Go away. Leave me alone."

"I'll never leave you my love! I have missed you too much."

"Please! Leave me alone."

"Sierra, do you want me to create a scene here and now? Your friends would not be too happy to hear about our history, would they? Why it would probably ruin your reputation. I imagine that would hurt your business in that lovely little shop wouldn't it."

"What do you want?"

"You my love,"

"Can we talk about this some other time?"

"You name the time and the place, but make it very soon. As you know, I'm not a patient man. You wouldn't want to get me riled up would you?"

"Please, tomorrow, out at the old farm house."

"Oh a fitting return to the scene of the crime. Wonderful! Make it early in the morning. Don't keep me waiting. Sweet dreams my lovely Sierra. Tell your gentleman friend that he is to keep his hands off of you or he might not like the consequences. Till the 'morrow then my love?"

He grabbed my hand and kissed the palm. A shudder went through my body. How could this have happened? How could he have found me? After all I did to be sure he would never know where I went. As quickly as he had appeared, he was gone. After several moments I wondered, had I just dreamt the past few minutes? No! My past had caught up with me.

Matt returned with the glass of punch and immediately realized that something was wrong.

"What happened Sierra? You're so pale. Who was that man that was talking to you? Did he say something to upset you?"

"No Matt. He just asked me to dance and I told him that I wasn't feeling well. He said he hoped that I felt better. I'm sorry Matt, but I have to go home. I really don't feel well. You stay and enjoy yourself. Please. I can walk home. It isn't that far."

"Oh no you don't. I'll drive you home. I'll even stay with you if you would like."

"No. I'll do better if I can be on my own. I'm sure that a good night's sleep will make me feel better. Promise me Matt that after you take me home you will come back to the party."

"Alright. I'll come back. But I won't enjoy myself. I'm sure sorry that you can't stay. We'll make up for it at the next dance."

"Thank you Matt. Now, please let's get out of here before Molly and Brad come back from the dance floor. I really don't want to have to explain again."

"Sure. No problem."

We made our way around the edge of the dance floor. Everyone seemed to want to talk to Matt, but we pushed on and finally made it outside the door. A young man quickly brought us the buggy and Matt helped me into the seat. He ran around and jumped up beside me. I felt as if I was in a daze. Nothing seemed real. In no time at all we were at my shop and Matt was helping me down. He did it very carefully and then guided me to my door. I was so afraid that he was going to kiss me, and I knew that I couldn't allow that to happen. Someone may be watching me. I dug in my purse for my key and rapidly opened the door.

"Matt, I'm so sorry. Good night."

"Sierra, are you sure you don't want me to stay with you for a while?"

"NO! Please Matt. Just leave me alone."

With that I was inside the shop slamming the door behind me. I couldn't contain myself any longer. I slumped to the floor and burst into tears. A rage I have never known seeped into every pore in my body.

"It can't be true. It just can't be true." I sobbed. "Just when I thought that I was safe. Dear god why?" I ranted and raved for what seemed like forever. My thoughts were not my own. Fear and terror had taken hold of me. I stayed that way for I don't know how long. Finally, I pulled myself to my feet and went into my bedroom. I knew I wouldn't sleep tonight. I knew that I would toss and turn and dread the coming morning.

"How can I possibly look at his face tomorrow? I won't go. I'll pack up a few things and leave here right now. He won't be able to find me. But, that's what I've been saying for a long time, and still he found me. The only thing I can do is try to reason with him. Reason? He doesn't know the meaning of the word. I'm caught in a trap. I can only go and hope that I can convince him to leave me alone. Maybe I can give him some money. Yes! He understands MONEY. But I really don't have a lot of money. Oh God, please, help me. What should I do?"

Sitting on the edge of the bed all night long, my mind racing, I kept trying to outguess this man that I had struggled so hard to leave behind. "I'll think of something. I have to or I'll go crazy."

The morning light began to glow over the hills in the distance. It came too soon. I rose from the bed and removed my beautiful dress. I donned a plain shirt and a long gabardine skirt. I pulled on my boots and wrapped a knitted stole around my shoulders. Methodically I walked to the door. I turned and glanced around my beautiful shop the shop that I had put together with my own two hands. I had felt safe here. Has it all been for nothing? Closing my mind of these thoughts, I opened the door and walked out onto the wooden sidewalk. It was just a short walk to the livery stable. It was very early and I had to wake the livery man.

He seemed shocked when I asked for a horse. I told him it would only be for a few hours. It was just a couple of minutes before I was in the saddle and heading out of town. I didn't want anyone to know where I was going, so I rode out in the opposite direction of where I was really going. I couldn't take a chance that someone might see me. After a couple of miles I reined the horse in the other direction and set off for my meeting. Each minute brought more dread into my heart. I wish Matt could have been beside me. He would have known what to do.

Chapter 12

Even at a slow pace it seems that I arrived at the farm too soon. I passed the sign 'Welcome Home Again Ranch'. Well, mom and pop, here I am. It's too late for you to know about it. I'll pay my respects to you both before I leave here today. Somehow I know that you're watching me. Please, Pop, help me through the nightmare that I know he will put me through. Why can't he just leave me alone?

I heard the faint sounds of horses and buggy wheels coming over the rise in the road. Even before I saw them, I felt my legs shaking uncontrollably. I remember when I saw this same scene years ago.

"Popie! Popie! I hear a wagon and horses coming. Maybe it's Doc Heller coming to pay a visit. Hurry, let's meet him."

"Alright See See, I'm coming. I swear you have the keenest ears I've ever known. I bet you can hear a blade of grass growing."

"Oh Popie, you're so silly. I can't do that. But I can hear the horses and wagon from a long way, away."

"Come on then. I'll race you to the front gate. Mom, better make sure we have some fresh coffee for Doc. You know how he loves a cup with your peach pie."

"Do you think he will bring me a piece of stick candy this time? Sometimes he forgets. But that's alright. He

probably came from the Patrick's farm. Mrs. Patrick is expecting a visit from the stork any day now."

"That's what that was! I wondered yesterday what that great big bird was that was flying around here. It's a good thing he knew this wasn't the right ranch. If he hadn't you may have had a new baby brother this morning."

"Oh Popie! Wouldn't that have been wonderful? I'm going to ask Doc if he can order me a baby brother. Wouldn't you like to have a baby?"

"Of course I would like to have a son, but I have my hands full right now with raising you. You take a lot of work and time you know. I don't know how I would have time to take care of a son."

"I wouldn't be a bother Popie. If we can order one from Doc I promise that I will be a good girl and do all my chores every day. Oh please! Let's ask him?"

"You two just sit here and finish your breakfast. I don't cook just because I love it you know? Doc can knock on the door. He's a big grown man." Mom was always teasing us about leaving the table too early.

"You never take time to digest your food before you two are gallivanting all over this farm. Now sit."

I quickly scooped up the last of my oatmeal and downed the milk from my glass. Pop was doing the same thing when the knock on the door came. I dashed over to open it, and was so surprised to find a total stranger standing there. Pop was beside me in an instant moving me behind him.

"Yes, young man, is there something we can do for you?"

"I'm so sorry to bother you sir, but I've been on the trail for several weeks and I used up all of the food and water that I kept in my buggy. I wonder if you would be so kind as to treat me to a meal and a canteen of water. I don't expect it for nothing. I would be happy to work for it."

"For goodness sake Pop, don't make the man stand there. Let him in." Mom had pushed pass Pop and was at the edge of the porch. "He could faint dead away before you put him into a chair. Please, mister, come in. We'll discuss payment after you've had a good breakfast. See See, run and get a wet cloth so that this man can clean his hands before he eats."

"I'm forever grateful for this kindness. I have never had to beg before, but I fell on some hard times. By the way, my name is Carl Ward. I know that I am not too far from Wild River Junction, but truthfully, I smelled your breakfast cooking and my stomach started making some pretty weird sounds."

"Where you heading Mr. Ward?"

"First of all, I thought I would see if I could find a buyer for my horses and wagon in town. Then maybe buy a single horse and saddle. Then if I'm lucky I should have a little money left over to continue my journey. I'm heading for Oregon. My sister and her husband live there and they tell me it's a good place to live. Seems there's work to be had there too. I didn't think as to how horses and a buggy would work in this trip, but I realize now that a single horse would be a better way to go."

"Oh, you're so right. After you eat, I'll take you into town and we'll talk to Gabe Rogers. He owns the livery stable. He'll know if there's anyone who is looking for a team and such."

Mr. Ward was able to woof down the mountain of a breakfast that mom cooked for him. There was a thick slice of ham from our own hogs and four eggs from our own chickens. The fluffiest biscuit's you'll ever eat made with mom's loving hands. And the gravy on top of them was made from Pop's homemade sausages and soo delicious. There was enough to cover everything even a second helping. He *drank four cups of coffee and when he was done, he pushed his plate aside and gasped.*

"Oh my lord! I don't think I have ever eaten anything so delicious. I can't believe I ate every crumb. Mrs. Rathburn, you are to be congratulated on your talent with a skillet. Mr. Rathburn, if you eat meals like that all the time I don't see why you don't weigh a ton. That meal was fabulous, and I thank you from the bottom of my heart."

"Now get along with you Mr. Ward. I bet your momma used to fix stuff like that for you."

"No, unfortunately, my momma died when I very small. My sister, the one in Oregon, raised me. She was just very young herself and couldn't boil water without burning it. We both had to learn to survive on the messes we made together. But survive we did. Now, Mr. Rathburn, what can I do to pay for my outstanding meal?"

"I tell you what Mr. Ward. Why don't we just head into town and see about selling your rig. Then if you have to wait for your buyer to come into town, you can come back here with me and we'll find something that you can do in the meantime. Maybe I can talk you into staying for a couple of days. I need some help right now in putting some fences around. I want to build a new corral, and things would go so much quicker if I had some help."

"But Popie? You said that I could help you."

"So you will. It's just that the more hands we have working on this, the quicker we can think about getting you your own pony."

"Oh, then let's ask mom to help too."

"And just who is going to be doing the cooking and cleaning if I'm out there hammering and sawing? I think not See See. Besides, you'd only have to redo whatever I did. I'm not good at that kind of work. Remember when Pop hung the gate? I nearly broke his arm. No. You just work with Popie."

I was very disappointed when Popie and Mr. Ward left for town and didn't ask me to go along. Mom said that it was because they were going to do men's work. But it sounded to me like they were going to have some fun. Like going to the livery stable and seeing all the horses that Mr. Rogers took care of. I finally accepted their rejection and lost myself in the chore of wandering the fields and picking wildflowers for mom.

When they returned Mr. Ward was astride a roan colored mare. She was very tall and had a stately air about her. Mr. Rogers had known of a buyer for the team and wagon and he had bought them on the spot. He made Mr. Ward a deal on his new horse and saddle and Mr. Ward was very happy with the swiftness of the sale. While on their journey to and from town, it had been decided that Mr. Ward would stay with us for two weeks. Pop had made him an offer regarding his pay and they were both very happy with the deal.

And so we began. Fencing was purchased, and the wire. I found it hard to keep up with both of them. Seems that Mr. Ward had been working on a ranch the year before and his main job was to string fence. I must admit, I was of no real help. I was able to bring them a tool from the wagon when they needed it or a drink of water. Any little thing that I felt helped. Pop told mom that I was the best assistant he had ever had. Mr. Ward said that they couldn't have worked so fast without me. I felt pretty proud. We were up before dawn each morning and drove out to the sight for the fence. Mom made sure that she had packed a big lunch for us in the picnic basket. We would take just a short time to gulp down the food and then it was back to the fence. I don't remember enjoying myself so much. Mr. Ward was a very funny person. He would make pop and me laugh so much.

One day when we finally neared the end of the fence project, Pop said that we had earned a long lunch break. He had asked mom to pack some extra things in our lunch basket, and it was a real celebration. We sat down on the tail gate of the wagon and enjoyed the treats that we found wrapped up in the blue linen cloth. After a while, Pop lay down inside the wagon and promptly fell asleep. Mr. Ward and I laughed, when Popsie's snoring began to sound like a pig snorting and then a whistling noise came from his throat. I had heard Pop snore before, but I had never been this close to him.

Mr. Ward suggested that he and I take a little walk and let Pop sleep. I told him that the fields were covered with wild flowers right now and that maybe we could pick some and take them home to mom. He thought that was a great idea. We wandered over a hill and were astounded at the beauty of the flowers. It was an array of blues, yellows and reds and all the shades in between. We picked a few flowers here and a few there. He said for me not to go out of his sight. He didn't want to lose me. Said he would have a hard time explaining to Mom and Pop that he had lost me in the field. I thought that was funny. After all, I had been in that field all my life. I knew that I wouldn't get lost. After we had picked several flowers, Mr. Ward came up to me and took my hand. We walked along together.

"Do you like me, See See?"

"Oh yes, Mr. Ward. I really like having you here."

"Good. Cause I like you, very much. I wish you were my little girl. Come here and let's sit on this log. Be careful. Don't scrape your knees on the bark. Better yet. Sit here on my lap. Now! Isn't that more comfortable?"

"Yes sir, Mr. Ward."

"Good, here, let me put my arms around you so that you don't fall. I like this don't you See See?"

"Ah! It's kinda too hot with your arms around me and you're squeezing me too tight. I can't breathe."

"No I'm not. Come on See See settle down. Let's just stay here like this for a little while. Look, see, I'm touching your leg and you're not hot. You have such soft skin. I love to touch it. Let me see if your face is as soft."

He pulled me close to his face and he kissed me on my cheek. I was very startled and decided that I didn't like it. I tried to pull away, but he held me fast and the next thing I knew, he was kissing me on my lips. I couldn't breathe. I was so startled. I started fighting him. He pulled away and laughed. I jumped down from his lap and picked up the flowers I had dropped while struggling with him.

"See See, there is nothing wrong with my kissing you. Everyone does that when they like each other. Doesn't your Pop and mom kiss?"

"Sometimes they do but not hard like that. I didn't like it. I couldn't breathe."

"All right my little one. I won't do that again. I'll wait until you're a grown up lady."

"I won't like it then either."

"Oh yes you will," he laughed. "You will be 'liking' it very much by then. Come on now. Your Pop will be waking up and wondering what's become of us. You better not tell him that you kissed me. He would be very upset and probably wouldn't get you a pony after all."

We made our way back to the wagon and Popie was just stirring.

"Hey you two! Wow! How long have I been asleep? I didn't realize I was that tired. I must have been out for a while. It was long enough for you to have picked all those flowers. They are lovely See See. I figure they are for mom and not for me."

"They're for both of you Popie. I'm sure glad you are awake though. Let's get back to work and finish the fence so

84

that we can start on the corral for my pony. I'm still getting a pony, right Popie?"

"Well have you been behaving yourself?"

I glanced over at Mr. Ward and he glared at me with dark eyes that made me very nervous.

"Oh, yes Popie. I've been real good and besides I helped you with the fence didn't I?"

"Well then, I guess I'll get you your pony."

The fence took until almost sundown before it was finished. Pop jumped up on the back of the wagon and surveyed the landscape. He was pleased with what he saw. The fence stood tall and straight.

"Good job Carl. I couldn't have done it without you. You sure you don't want to stay for a couple more weeks? I could sure use you."

"No George. I'll have to leave just as soon as we finish the corral. But I really appreciate all that you and Mrs. Rathburn have done for me. "

"Well, so be it then. I know your sister is anxious to see you. Heaven knows you have a long journey ahead of you. So anyway, we have to drive into town tomorrow and buy some more hardware for the corral. Darn! Wish I could have thought about buying it the other day when we bought the fence posts. We could have got a head start on the corral."

"Well hey George. It doesn't take both of us to go to town. Why don't I start things here and you go to town on your own."

"That sounds like an idea. But how about you go into town and I get things started. I know exactly what I want to do to that area and I could have a lot done by the time you get back. It sure would save time."

"That's alright with me George. Maybe I could have some company on my trip. See See, how about going with

me? Maybe we can see that pony of yours if it's been delivered to Mr. Rogers."

I was torn between the bad feeling I had about what had transpired between Mr. Ward and I and the exciting knowledge that my pony might be in town and I could see it. I hesitated for a moment and I guess that Popie picked up on it because he said that if I didn't want to go I didn't have to. But the excitement won out and I said that I would go.

Just after sunrise the next morning I awoke with a feeling that it was to be a very exciting day. Quickly I dressed and went into the kitchen. Pop and Mr. Ward were already seated at the table and mom was standing over the stove, cooking up her usual wonders. The men were talking about what was needed from town and mom asked me if I could remember to go to the general store and buy a spool of black thread. She gave me a little purse and said that the money inside would be enough for the thread and if there was any left over I could buy myself a stick of hard rock candy. I couldn't believe my ears. What an exciting day this was to be. Not only would I get to see my pony, but I'd get hard rock candy too. Could my life get any better?

Pop and Mr. Ward hitched up the wagon and it was pulled around to the front door.

"Your chariot awaits my lady." Popie said with a big grin on his face. "Now you mind Mr. Ward See See. You're doing a very grown up thing by going shopping for your mother. We are very proud of you. Now, up you go and hold on tight. I don't want you falling off half way into town. We're so busy, that Mr. Ward might not have time to pick you up until he comes back down the road later on this afternoon. Then you would have missed out seeing your pony, if it is there yet, and the rock candy."

"Yes Popie. I will be good and thank you for trusting me to do this errand. I love you and momma very much."

"We love you too See See. Now Mr. Ward, don't get losing my girl. Be sure you bring her back. Get going now you two."

Pop watched us as we rode out of sight. It was a warm morning and the sun was already heating up the world.

We had gone only a couple of miles when Mr. Ward turned the team in the wrong direction. I couldn't understand why. He had been into town with Popsi several times. He surely knew the way. All he had to do was to follow the road. But here we were going across a field and there was no trail to follow.

"Where are you going Mr. Ward? The town is over there. You should have stayed on the road. Popsi will be upset when he finds out you went somewhere else."

"There is no doubt my love. He will be a little unhappy but you and I are about to go on an adventure. Just you and I. Just the two of us. I promise you that we will have lots of fun."

"No! I don't want to go on an adventure. I want to go into town and see my pony and get my rock candy. You promised me."

"Well my dear See See, you have to learn that we can't always have the things we want. Sometimes we have to change our plans."

Sitting still on the wagon, I saw mile after mile pass under the wheels. Too scared to say anything I sat in total silence. After what seemed like hours, we came to some rail road tracks. He pulled the wagon just beyond the tracks and we stopped. In the distance I could hear the whistle of a train and as it got closer I watched it slow down. It was in front of us now, chugging to a stop.

"Good. The train is going to take on water right here. Come my little one. We are going for a long train ride. How *exciting. Just you and I, traveling afar. We have our whole life ahead of us. Our future is well in hand."*

He lifted me down from the wagon and pulled me along to the train. I tried to resist, but my little form was nothing compared to his size. He lifted me into the doorway and stepping up on the metal steps he followed me. We walked into a car and he found two seats at the back. He pushed me into the seat by the window and he sat very close, next to me. I sat in silent terror. I couldn't understand what was happening but I knew it wasn't right. How would mom and Popie know where I was? Why had Mr. Ward not gone into town? He knows we had promised to come home safely. Where are we going?

Chapter 13

Pop used to say that a person should always be their best because it was a well known fact that life goes in circles. What happens today will be something we will probably be doing years from now. I used to laugh at him. How could something I'm doing right now come back to haunt me? How right he was. Here I stand in my old home watching a horse and wagon come up over the rise. Only this time I know it's the devil that's coming.

The wagon pulled in front of the broken down gate and came to a stop. He got down from the seat and loosely wound the reins around the stand. Slowly he walked down the overgrown path and entered the doorway. A self satisfied smug expression was on his face. He looked at me with those dark eyes and I felt a shudder run down my spine.

"Well my lovely one. Here we are again. How ironic that we are back here on the farm where it all started. Kind' a like it was meant to be. Do you know how long I've been looking for you? You probably thought you were safe after all this time. I just knew that my cousin would be able to find out where you were if he kept an eye on Annie. Oh! You probably didn't know that I knew where Annie was did you?"

He had to be bluffing. There was no way he could have found Annie. No one knew that I had left her with Arletta. No one!

"You're trying to trick me. You don't know where Annie is. I made sure that the trail would never lead you to her. There is no way your stupid cousin could have found her."

"Oh, believe me my love, he did find her. My cousin is a very persuasive man. If he uses his charms there isn't anything that you stupid women won't tell him. He was especially 'kind' to that fat bitch Marlene you worked with for so many years. She spilt the beans about everything. How you saved enough money to make a trip to another location and planned to start your own business. How you left Annie with Arletta Daniels until you could send for her. It just took time for him to be able to find out where you had gone. He broke into her house one night while she was away and he found a letter from you telling everything we needed to know. So, here I am in Wild River Junction. Now! Don't I deserve a warm welcome from my wife after all that I have done to find her?"

He expected a warm welcome? How could he possibly believe that I would be welcoming him? I had spent so many years trying to get away from him. I just couldn't believe he had found me. It scares me that he knows where Annie is. But he seems to know everything that I have worked so hard to keep him from finding out. I really thought I could trust Marlene with my secret. I guess you never really know people. She always was a sucker for a smooth talking man.

"Carl, I don't know what you expect from me. Doesn't my running away let you know that I don't want to be with you?"

"Well, my love, I must admit that it hurt my feelings a little bit. The more I was able to find out, the more fun I began to have. Now, just come over here and give me a warm welcome and I will forgive you – maybe. Come on! Just cross over this floor and everything will be as it was before."

Everything as before? How could he imagine that I would want to go back to that? All the beatings he gave me and the sexual abuse. Times he forced me to steal. Never! Never would I submit to that again.

"Ward, I came out here to meet you because I did not want anyone in town to see us together. I came to tell you that it is over. I will not go back with you. I have another life that I am living now and I won't give it up. How could you even imagine that I would be happy to see you? My life with you was nothing but starvation and abuse. Go away and leave me alone. I am no longer your wife."

The blackness that crossed over his face put the fear of God in me. I've seen that look before, but never as intense as it was this time.

"Do you really believe that I came all this way for nothing? You are my wife. You will always be my wife and nothing you do or say will change that. Now I would like to do this quietly and calmly but if necessary it will happen with force."

He bounded across the room in a flash and I was held in his vice grip. He was so much bigger and stronger than I. I fought hard but to no avail. He reached out and grabbed hold of the top of my dress and ripped it. My breasts were exposed and he grabbed at them with his worn, rough hands and squeezed until I gasped from the pain.

"See, Sierra. You have forgotten how much you enjoy that. Now settle down and let us try to enjoy that which is inevitable. Stop fighting me. You know you won't win."

He held me tight and suddenly I found my arms locked behind my back. He put his lips on my nipple bit hard and sucked. I could only scream from the pain and the humiliation. There was nothing I could do to stop this. As always he overpowered me. He picked me up and threw me down on the dusty floor. Standing over me he removed his belt and began to unbutton his pants. He paused for a moment and shook the belt at my head. Then he dropped it on the floor beside me.

"Watch me Sierra. Watch me as I undress just for you my love. You know you're looking forward to what I have to offer you. You always pretended not to like it, but I know you did. Watch me while I let loose this magnificent staff that will bring you such joy."

"No Ward, you can't do this. Please! I have a new life now. Please! Let me be. Leave me alone." I begged him knowing that it would never be as I wanted it. He had me now, where he wanted me. Lying on my back, knowing that no matter what I said or tried to do I could not stop this rape that was about to occur. I started to squirm, to get out from under him. I saw his hand fly out in a flash and I felt the pain on my cheek. He started to laugh, as only he can laugh. In an instant he ripped the rest of my dress from my body. My undergarments were shredded. He was then on top of me, holding my hands so that I couldn't fight back. With his knees he spread my legs apart and painfully he entered me.

I tried to be somewhere else in my mind. It was something I used to be able to do when he forced himself on me before, but this time I couldn't do it. He grunted and howled and made his usual noisy sounds of pleasure. It seemed forever before he climaxed, his body slapping against mine, grinding me into the floor. Then he was finished. He was spent. He rolled over and lay down beside me, his arm over my breast. No words were spoken for a long time, until, "Sierra my love, you are still the most beautiful love of my life. I have missed you so much. More than you will ever know. I will never let you go again. You are mine forever. We will go and get Annie and make a new life for the three of us."

Knowing that nothing I could say would dissuade him at this moment I decided to play along with him and pretend that he was right.

"Yes, Ward, we could do that. But I have to go back into town and pack up all my things and sell my merchandise. It shouldn't take too long. Can I do that?"

"Sierra, do you really think that I would let you go back into that town where you have so many friends? I'm not stupid you know. You're not going anywhere. We're going to stay out here for a couple of days and then we will take off for parts unknown. Nobody would think of looking for us out here. Let them think that you decided to leave town and not tell anyone. "

He stood up and dressed himself all the while his eyes never left me. Then he reached down and pulled me to my feet. He pulled me to the ladder that lead to the attic and forcefully pushed me up the rungs. In the attic he steered me to the bed and gave me a push. He grabbed hold of my hand and pulled it up to the headboard. Taking a section of rope from his pocket he tied my hand. Then, all the time smiling, he tied my other hand. I was petrified. He had me in such a situation that I would never be able to get free to get help. Dear God, what would become of me now?

Chapter 14

The doors to the saloon swung open and Matt burst through. He looked around the empty room and walked over to the bar.

"Hey Boots! Where's Molly?"

"She went to see how Docs doing."

"What's wrong with Doc?"

"Oh he slipped and fell down some steps the other day. He was visiting one of his patients. He kind'a hurt his ankle. Molly's been checking up on him every day to make sure he keeps his foot up. She says that Doc is one of the worst kind of patients."

"She's probably right. Well maybe I'll go by and see him too. Thanks Boots."

Matt walked down the street and glanced over his shoulder. Sierra's place was still closed. Something wasn't right. He had knocked on her door several times and got no response. She was always open by now. In fact a couple of ladies had stopped him and asked if he knew when Sierra's Finery would be open. He couldn't help them. He was afraid that she was sick, but it seems she would have at least answered his pounding on the door. Maybe she was *really* sick. It had all seemed so strange how she had left the dance in a hurry on Saturday night. She sure hadn't seemed to be herself. He'd ask Doc when he saw him. Maybe Molly knew what was going on. He needed to find the answers. After all, he was the Sheriff. If anyone was missing he should be informed about it. While walking down the street and up onto the sidewalk, he thought about the night of the dance. The change had happened so fast. One minute Sierra was happy and laughing and the next she was feeling ill. At least she said she felt ill. She looked more scared than ill. It had happened right after that stranger walked over and talked to her. Matt wondered if he had said anything to offend her. Next time he spoke to Sierra he would ask her who that man was. Matt realized that he had never seen the man either before the dance or since then. He made a mental note to investigate it. Somebody in town must know who he was.

Walking up to Doc's door, Matt opened it up and walked into the office. Neither Doc nor Molly was in sight.

"Hello! Anybody here?"

He heard a scurrying of feet coming from upstairs, then the clomp clomp of shoes on the stairway. Molly always wore those high heeled shoes. He recognized the sound of them right away. The swishing of her gown as it brushed the stair railing made the sound of the wind blowing through the weeping willow tree down by the river. As always she had a smile on her face.

"Matt! Don't tell me you need to see Doc. Did you get shot or something?"

"No Molly. I'm really looking for you. But how is Doc? Heard he got himself messed up a little. Is he going to live? Should I call the undertaker and order a pine box for him."

A rough voice echoed down the stairs as to what Matt could do with the pine box. Doc stated that he would outlive that tin star bum and he would be the one ordering the box.

"Now see what you've done Matt. You've upset Doc. I just had a set too with him before you got here. I found him walking up the stairs. He'll never heal that ankle if he doesn't keep off of it. You men are all alike. You know what you should do, but damned if you're going to do it. Talk about hard headed. "

"Sorry about that. Someday I'll learn to keep my mouth shut. But hey, Molly, there's something I need to talk to you about. Have you seen Sierra? I've been by her shop several times and she doesn't seem to be around. I know she was feeling poorly last Saturday so I figured that she would rest up on Sunday, but here it is Monday and she hasn't opened her shop yet. I banged on her door but got no response. You got any idea where she is?"

"No! I noticed this morning that there were several ladies waiting outside her shop, but I didn't think too much of it. If she is ill, she would keep the shop closed until she was well. Let's go up and ask Doc if he has seen her."

Following Molly up the stairs, Matt found himself feeling something was about to happen. You know, like when you get a cold shudder run up your spine for no apparent reason. There used to be a saying that it was someone walking over your grave. Molly entered the first room on the left giving a brief knock on the door that stood open. Doc was sitting in a big arm chair under the window with his foot up on a padded stool. With the light coming in from the window you could almost imagine a halo of light around his head. But when you looked at Doc's face you could see that it was impossible for it to be a halo.

"How in the hell am I supposed to get any rest when I'm plagued with people running in and out at their whim. I'm trying to catch up on some of my medical papers. Why don't you two just go back down the stairs and out the door and lock it after yourselves. I don't want to see you for a week."

"I don't care what you want you old crone. I'm coming by a couple times a day to be sure you behave yourself. No more walking around. I'll bring you your meals and a pitcher of water so that you have no reason to get up except to go to bed. That's where you should be anyway. But I'll settle for this chair. Now Doc we have something important to ask you. Have you seen Sierra in the past couple of days? Did she maybe come by and talk to you about not being well?"

"No. I haven't seen her. Is she ill?"

"Well she left the dance early on Saturday night because she wasn't feeling well. I expected to see her in church on Sunday morning but she wasn't there. I figured she was resting at home. But I went by her shop and she didn't answer the door. She didn't even open her shop today. Something strange is going on. Did you by any chance happen to see a stranger moving around town? With you sitting by that window I figure you can see everything that's going on."

"There was someone driving a wagon early yesterday morning. I thought at the time that it was no one I recognized. He looked a lot like that man that was at the dance on Saturday night. He was tall, grim, with a black beard and mustache. That sound like the one you're talking about?"

"Yeah! Exactly like him. Do you know who he is Molly?"

"Don't have an inkling. I did see him at the dance. But he didn't stay too long. I believe he talked to Sierra for a while. He left right after that. Why Matt? Something about this man bothering you?"

"Yeah. I don't know why, but I get this bad feeling about him. Oh well, might be something I ate. But getting back to Sierra, what do you think we should do? Surely if she was really ill she would have contacted Doc. You don't suppose she is so bad off that she can't get out of bed do you?"

"Matt, I don't know what to think, but I tell you what we're going to do. I'm going back to the saloon and get the spare key that I have for her shop. If she doesn't answer the door this time we'll use the key and go inside. In fact, you stay outside and I'll go in. If she is indisposed, she sure as hell isn't going to want you to see her that way."

"Molly, that sounds like a great plan. Alright Doc, we're leaving you now. You can study your papers. About time you learned some new things anyway."

"Thank God! Finally I get a little peace and quiet. All joking aside, let me know what you find out about Sierra. If she is sick, just let me know and I'll come running. Or better yet I'll come hobbling on my crutches. Just keep me informed."

"You bet Doc. Molly will come back and let you know."

With a sense of relief and yet a feeling of urgency, both Matt and Molly left Doc's house and made their way to Sierra's Finery. The shop was still closed up tight and the blinds were still lowered. Matt knocked on the door. Gently at first, but each knock echoed louder and louder as the silence from inside the shop became deafening. Molly realized that it was no use and she ran up the street into the saloon.

It seemed like hours to Matt before Molly returned. She'd had trouble finding the key. She knew she had put it in a safe place where she would always be able to find it; unfortunately it wasn't where she thought she had put it. Finally she discovered it. Once more they knocked and once more no response. So Molly unlocked the door and walked into the shop. What was left of daylight lit her way to the back of the shop where Sierra's living quarters were. She called out. Still no response. Knocking on the door she entered and looked around.

The bed had been made up and everything was neat and clean. The dress she had worn to the dance was hanging in the wardrobe. There didn't seem to be a lot of clothes missing, like if she had gone off on a trip. Just one hanger was empty. The dancing slippers were up on the top shelf. So, Sierra had been in the shop long enough to change her clothes, but had she slept here? Walking into the kitchen she saw one cup and saucer setting in the sink. Not much of a clue though. Sierra could have set it there before she dressed for the dance. But where could she have gone? She didn't own a horse or a wagon so she either went with someone, or she walked. Spending a little time walking around the area Molly decided that something just didn't feel right. She figured that she should go outside to Matt and maybe between the two of them they could come up with something. She sure wasn't having any luck inside.

"Matt, I'm stumped. She isn't inside. I don't know what to think. She must have walked to wherever she was going, or got a ride from someone. But who? It isn't like her to just go and leave her shop. She worked so hard to get it open. And why didn't she let us know she was going away for a while? The only thing missing in her clothes wardrobe is one outfit. I don't know which one it is, but one of the hangers is empty. If she had gone away for a couple of days, she surely would have taken more clothes with her. I just don't like the feel of this."

"Yeah Molly, I know what you mean. She would never leave for any length of time knowing that she had customers coming on Monday morning. The mayor's wife said she had an appointment with her at 10:00 a.m. for a new hat fitting. I'm going to walk around town and ask some questions. Maybe someone saw her. Why don't you go to the saloon and ask some questions there. Maybe between the two of us we can figure out what happened. I'll meet you in the saloon just as soon as I make the circle of town."

"Alright Matt. That's a good idea. Let's not worry about her until we know we have something to worry about."

As she was about to lock the shop door Molly decided to take one last look around. She wondered where Sierra could be. Everything in the shop and the living area was as neat as pin. If someone had entered the shop and taken Sierra with them, then she went willingly. Nothing seems to have been disturbed. Just one more glance around, and a peek outside the back door. Nothing! It was a real mystery. Alright, she would high tail it down to the saloon and start asking around. She just felt that between her and Matt, they would be getting some answers to this riddle.

Matt walked with a confident air as he strolled down the main street. Someone must have seen her and he was going to find out. After visiting several of the shops and offices down the main street he began to lose some of his enthusiasm. Nobody had seen Sierra since the dance. They all offered their own explanation as to what might have happened.

"Maybe she wanted some peace and quiet and took off for the river."

"Maybe some long lost friend found her and they wanted to be alone and had gone to Overton. (I hear the new hotel there is real swanky.)"

Matt had rejected each idea. He just couldn't believe she would just leave without at least leaving a note. He was about to run out of shops on the south side of the street and it was beginning to get dark. Several of the store owners were beginning to take down their signs and put the display merchandise inside their shops.

Matt knew that he would never be able to cover all the territory in time this evening. Well, there was one place he could inquire at. At the end of the street was the livery stable and old Gabe Rogers would still be there. He never seemed to close. No wonder he was so good at his job. He had a good reputation for treating animals well if they were boarded with him, or you could count of the truth about an animal if you bought one from him. Gabe was inside one of the stalls brushing down a roan mare. I don't know who seemed to enjoy it the most, Gabe or the mare.

"Hey Sheriff! What you doing down this end of town this late in the afternoon? Somebody report a stolen horse and you figure I had it here?" Gabe had a way of talking with a smile on his face and a bubbly laugh to accompany it. He knew darned well that he was safe. Matt would never think he was involved with anything illegal.

"Gabe. I heard there was a real lively chicken fight going on behind your barn. Thought I might bet a couple of dollars on it. You know how poorly us lawmen are paid. I have to make extra money any way I can."

"If I had such a thing happening Matt I would have put a big sign up on the front of my building. Not much use having chickens fight if there is only you and me watching it."

"Too true. Seriously Gabe, have you by any chance seen anything of Sierra Martin in the past couple of days? She was at the dance on Saturday night and now no one has seen her since. We're starting to get a little concerned."

"Now that you mention it, I did see her. It was just after dawn yesterday morning. She had walked down from her shop and I was kidding her about not having gone home from the dance yet. She took one of my horses and lit out of here like her feet were on fire."

"What direction did she go Gabe?"

"Oh, let me see. I'm pretty sure she went east. Hmm! I had forgotten about that. Guess I'm getting old. I nearly forgot that's one of my horses that hasn't come home yet. She said she would have it back sometime during the day, but I never saw her or the horse."

"Did she give you any idea where she was going? Was there anyone with her?"

"No. She was by herself and I never ask questions of a beautiful lady. She was dressed to ride. She had on a shirt and a long skirt, boots on her feet and a knitted thing around her shoulders. It was mighty chilly that early in the morning and I remember thinking she was going to get cold before she had gone very far. Don't know what there is east of town. Maybe she just wanted to ride to clear out the old brain. Course, if she didn't come back, maybe something happened to her. If she had fallen off the horse, it would have high tailed it back here. Don't rightly know what to tell you Matt."

"Thanks Gabe. You've been a big help. I guess its too late tonight to go looking for her, but the first thing in the morning I will. I'll get a couple of guys to help. If she comes back before dawn, let me know."

"Sure will. Good luck Matt."

Matt almost ran down the main street. He hadn't really wanted to hear about Sierra leaving town, but he had. Where could she have gone? Why did she go in an easterly direction? Why would she leave so early in the morning? Maybe she didn't want anyone to see her leave. But why?

Not getting any answers from himself to his questions, Matt sped up. He glanced in the direction of Sierra's Finery and realized that he was really worried about her. He had grown so used to seeing some kind of light on in the shop. It now looked so abandoned and cold.

"I don't know where you are Sierra, but I'll find you. I promise you that." He caught himself saying it out loud.

As he rounded the corner and neared the saloon he could hear the rinky dink piano being played with much vigorous energy. The old keys were being struck with all the enthusiasm the player could muster. Pushing the swinging door in Matt walked over to the bar and asked Boots for a drink.

"Hey Matt! I thought you had given up drinking."

"Yeah, well, I had. But right now I feel a need for one drink. Where's Molly?"

"I'm right behind you bad boy. What's with this drinking thing? You said you had gone on the wagon and nothing would ever make you get off."

"Well, something has caused me to change my mind. I found out that Sierra rented a horse from Gabe real early yesterday morning. She told him she would be back sometime in the afternoon. She didn't return. Could be something happened to her on the trail. He said that his horse would have come back on its own if Sierra had fallen off. I can only assume that she and the horse are in some kind of trouble. I can't look for her in the dark so I'll have to wait until the morning before I go searching. This is going to be a long night, that's for sure."

"Which direction did she go?"

"Easterly."

"What in the hell is east of here except a lot of dirt? Boots, give me the same thing that Matt's having and give him another one."

"Thanks Molly, but one is enough. I want my head clear when I go searching for her. I just keep getting this bad feeling."

"I know what you mean. I asked everyone here if they had seen her, but no one had. It's like she went out on a puff of smoke."

"Well Molly, I'm going to go back to the office and do some paper work and then get me some shut eye. I want to leave before the sun comes up. I need to find a couple of fellows to go with me. The more people looking the sooner we'll find her. If she comes home tonight on her own I'm going to give her a piece of my mind. That is what's left of it."

"Take it easy cowboy. I know you're anxious about her, so am I, but we need to keep our heads clear. If she does come back I just know she will have a good explanation as to what happened and where she has been. Go back to your office and keep yourself busy. When you get back tomorrow I expect a full accounting of what went on. You'll find her Matt. I just know you will."

Hoping against hope that Molly was right, Matt walked down toward the Sheriff's office. On the way he stopped by Smitty Cohan's house and asked him if he and his son would go with him tomorrow. He knew they would. They had never turned him down before. They were a great team. Smitty had been a scout in his younger days and was always happy to hone up his expertise. It was decided that they would leave before daylight. Matt sat at his desk for a couple of hours and found himself just pushing the papers around. Nothing got done. Finally, he walked into the back, went inside one of the empty jail cells and laid down on the bunk. Hours later he was still turning and tossing. If he didn't get any sleep he wouldn't be fit for anything. Finally, he drifted off. He hadn't been asleep for long when there was a pounding sound. Startled, he jumped up and sleepily opened the door.

"Alright Matt. It's time to go. You told me to wake you up just before dawn and here I am."

"Thanks Smitty. I could have sworn I just went to sleep."

Grabbing his boots, hat and guns Matt joined the Cohan's. Thank God at last they could start the search for Sierra.

The early morning brought a chill to the air as they rode alongside each other. Heading east out of town there was little conversation. Smitty was keeping his keen eye on the road looking for some sign that she had come this way. Gabe had told Matt that the left rear shoe on his horse had a small nick on the outside, so it would be easy to recognize when they found the trail. Traveling for several hours, watching the sun rise up over the hills and bring a little warmth to them, Matt realized that nowhere had they seen any trace of

Sierra's horse. There had not been any rain or even a wind so they couldn't have eliminated the tracks on the trail. The weather had been very balmy for this time of the year. Matt had hoped that they would discover her tracks as soon as they left town. It was determined that they would continue on until sunset and if there was nothing by then, they would camp over night and then continue in the morning. But how far would they go?

"We'll decide in the morning." Matt told them.

Chapter 15

Molly had prowled around town for hours, which in a town the size of Wild River took some real doing. In the course of conversations with each person she encountered she hoped that they had not noticed that her mind was not on the subject at hand. She had admired the new dishes that Mr. Bellman had shown her. They were bone white, with a row of bright red, tiny English roses. Each dish edged with a thin band of gold. You could almost see through the dish. The shadow of your hand reflected through with the sunlight. Any other time she would have Oo'ed and Ah'ed about them, but not today. This was the third day that Matt had been gone. Nobody knew anything as to where they had gone. She could only hope that Matt would be coming down the street any moment bringing Sierra along with him.

In a setting like Wild River Junction, it doesn't take long to become very attached to someone. Even though Molly had only known Sierra for a few months, she had instinctively taken a liking to her. She had given the distinct impression that she was a hard working, honest and loving person. Molly had never seen anyone work as hard as Sierra had in cleaning and repairing that old building. She had done most of it herself too. Sure, she had had young Pat Grady to help, but most of it was of her own volition. What a great job she had done too. The shop looked so delicate. A place that any woman would feel excited to enter. Not too many places like that in these here parts. Even in Overton there was nothing like it. Overton was a much larger town, but not a shop anything like Sierra's. Makes you wonder why she decided to settle in Wild River. Not half as many people as in Overton. Oh well! How lucky we are to have her here.

"Hey, Molly! Have you heard anything from Matt yet?" Gabe Rogers hollered across the street.

"No, Gabe. Nothing yet! I'm trying not to worry, but after all this time I can't help but wonder what happened."

"Oh, old Matt will find her. They'll be coming down that trail any minute now."

"Thanks' for keeping my spirits up, Gabe. I'll let you know when I learn something. Of course you'll probably know before me. They'll be returning your horse."

Molly wandered down to Doc's office and entered the doorway. His ankle was a lot better now, and he was able to open his office up this morning. He was using his crutches, but at least he could help the couple of people that had need of him. Most of Doc's patients lived outside of town, but sometimes they would come by to see him if they were picking up supplies or such. It was well known that Doc had one time traveled 24 hours straight to reach someone that needed him. He was a good doctor too. He pretended to be so hard and acted grouchy, but he had a real soft heart. He'd chew your butt out one minute and the next he would be arriving at your place with a bowl of soup he fixed or a bunch of flowers to make you feel better. Yes, he was a good man.

"Mrs. Baxter. How are you today? It looks like that baby is about to pay us a visit."

"Yes Molly. I will be so happy when she gets here. She's been so much more active than my two boys were. She kicks all the time."

"You know it's a girl?"

"Yep! Doc promised that this one would be a girl and I never knew Doc to break a promise. Excuse me Molly, I 'm next to go in."

"Good luck Mrs. Baxter."

Molly waited for a half an hour before she decided to leave Doc's office. He was pretty busy and she didn't want to slow him down.

She walked back out into the street and glanced down at Sierra's place. It looked so lonely and abandoned. Deciding to go back to the saloon the back way and maybe passing the time with a couple of the guys playing poker, Molly didn't seem to have any enthusiasm to do anything. She hated this waiting. But then, no news would bring her no bad news. She walked down the alley and at the end she turned to her left. She felt that she could walk these streets and alley ways with her eyes closed; she had done it so many times. The early evening air was cooling off the day. She knew that it wouldn't be long before winter got here. She gave a little shudder, thinking about the cold and the wind that was bound to be upon them. Pushing the swinging doors in, she entered the saloon and walked over to the tables.

"Alright! Where's the lucky man that's going to try and take my money today?"

A murmur went through the room and several men stood up, scraping the chair legs on the old wooden floor.

Not too often would Molly instigate a card game. They all knew what was going on in her mind. They knew that even though her thoughts were not on what she was doing, they would more than likely lose. She could read those cards before they were dealt. At least that's what everyone said, but not a soul would even intimate that Molly cheated. She didn't have to. She had been taught by the best. Her daddy had played on the River Queen down in New Orleans for a lot of years. She would sit on his lap as he dealt the cards. They said that Molly's first word was 'Deal'. But if old

Molly needed a distraction, there were a few people that would volunteer to be fleeced. She always made it up to them when they lost. Molly was a good old girl, and loved by more than she would ever know.

"Alright Boots. Bring a pitcher of beer over to me and my lambs. Order some sandwiches too. I'm kind'a hungry and I know they won't let me eat alone. We're going to be here all night I reckon."

"Will do Molly. Let me know when you need anything else."

The card game went on for several hours. It wasn't a cut throat kind of game, just a fun one. Each of the men left the table one by one as they lost the few dollars that they felt they could lose, but their places were taken by fresh meat. Molly was, of course, winning and the chips pilled up in front of her. Suddenly realizing that she was tired she called a halt to the game and excused herself while listening to the cries of the men who wanted to get their money back and about how Molly couldn't quit while she was ahead. She'd heard it all before many times, but this time she realized that there wasn't the anger in their threats that there could have been. Everyone was waiting with her for any kind of news.

"Goodnight boys! Old Molly is dead tired tonight so I can't entertain you any longer. Thanks for my bank roll. Boots, be sure to lock up after everyone goes. See you in the morning. And thanks boys, for being here tonight."

A round of good nights rumbled through the room and they all watched as Molly walked up the stairs. She still had that special thing about her that everyone had always loved. She was no spring chicken anymore but by golly, she was one hell of a woman. As she disappeared down the hall, the sound of men's voices echoed across the room. There wasn't one of them that didn't respect the lady that had just left the room. Some would probably even go home and dream about her tonight. What a gal!

Molly settled herself at her dressing table. Looking at the image in the mirror she could easily see the bags under the eyes and the wrinkles around her mouth. Feeling about one hundred years old, she scanned the image she was looking at.

"One of these days I'm going to have to give serious thoughts about giving up this kind of work. Each day I can see one or two more gray hairs and three more wrinkles. I wonder if the young girls know how lucky they are to have such firm and smooth skin. I bet they don't think twice about it, but then I guess that I didn't when I was young. You just believe that it will always look that way. I can still keep up my end of the dancing and such, but, for how much longer? After all, next month I'm going to be – Oh quit whining. Just get this layer of paint off your face and go to bed. Sleep is what you want you silly old biddy. Hey, stop calling my good friend names. Oh, wow! I'm talking to myself. Maybe my mind is going now as well as my body. I'll pay attention to that fact in the morning. I'm too tired tonight. Good night old girl."

It was just as the sun was beginning to come up over the far horizon that, if you listened carefully you could hear the sound of horse hooves plodding down the street. They were so quiet that no one in town heard them. That was good. Matt didn't want to have to tell everyone that they had failed in the search.

Chapter 16

"Hey, dam it Matt, wake up and open this door!" The spectators near by could hear the urgency in Molly's voice. "It's nearly noon. I've given you plenty of time to rest, now open up." She pounded hard and the door rattled on its hinges.

She had been startled awake early this morning by one of the old cow hands that hung around the saloon and helped out with the sweeping and such. She was ready to give him what for when he announced that Matt and the Cohan's were back. Said that he had passed the Sheriff's office and saw the Sheriff's horse tied to the post out front. He had tried the door, but it was locked. He knew that Molly wanted to be informed the minute Matt was back and so he had high tailed it to the saloon and knocked on Molly's door.

Hurriedly she had dressed, and left the saloon by the back door. It was only moments later that she was outside the Sheriff's office and knocking on the door. But, no one answered. Gabe hollered from across the street that they had got in just a couple of hours ago and that they hadn't had any sleep for twenty four hours.

"Why don't you let them sleep for an hour or two longer before you shake the building again." Old Gabe stated.

Realizing that Gabe had a point, Molly had returned to the saloon and waited. She ate breakfast, checked the inventory behind the counter and counted the money in the safe. Things she did every day. Things that seem to take up such a big part of her day, but today, they seemed to be accomplished quickly. She went up to her rooms, and took time to bathe, dress with care and put on her makeup. Continually looking at the old clock that hung on the wall it seemed that time stood still. Finally, it had been three hours since she had first been told about Matt's return.

Walking out of the swinging doors and looking down the street, she noticed that Sierra's Finery was still closed and the blinds were still down. Was she sleeping? Maybe she felt she had to stay closed today in order to get enough rest. Oh well, Matt would let her know what happened.

Reaching the front door to the Sheriff's office Molly peered into the window. The blind was still down and no sound came from within. "Well, if he thinks I'm waiting any longer, he's got another thought coming." she said to herself.

"Hey, Matt, open up." After what seemed like forever, she heard boots scraping across the floor and the bolt being pulled on the door. The bearded, scruffy looking individual that opened the door only bore a slight resemblance to the Matt she knew. His blood shot eyes almost bore holes through her.

"God Molly, why don't you make a little bigger ruckus? There might be a couple of people in the outlaying farms that didn't hear you."

"You're lucky I didn't break the window and climb through."

"Now I would have paid money to see that, seeing as there are bars on the windows. I reckon about ten inches tween the bars. How do you think you would have crammed all of that between them?" He playfully pointed to her back side.

"Alright, no need to be rude."

"Sorry Molly. It's just that we had such little sleep for the past three and a half days. I was dog tired. Come on in and I'll make some coffee."

"Wash your face and comb your hair while you're at it too. You look scary as hell. Now I know why no woman ever wanted to marry you. If she saw you looking like that first thing every morning it would scare her off."

"Just sit here and I'll go in the back and freshen up a bit. Maybe by then my brain will be able to work enough to tell you what happened, or rather, what didn't happen."

"What do you mean, what didn't happen? You did find Sierra didn't you? Come on, never mind the spoofing up, tell me what happened!"

"It will only take me five minutes. By then the coffee will be ready and we can sit."

Men can be so darned ornery sometimes Molly thought. I don't understand why he couldn't just keep quiet for two more minutes before he dropped that rock on my head. I don't like the way it sounded. What didn't happen? Does that mean that they didn't find Sierra? The knot in Molly's stomach told her that whatever Matt told her was not going to be good news.

"Gosh darn, Matt. What's taking you so long? I'm giving you one more minute and then I'm coming back there. You ain't got nothing I've never seen before anyway."

"Yeah, but you never seen anything like what I have to offer."

"Dream on little man!"

By the time the banter back and forth was over, Matt walked into the office. He looked some better, still needed a shave, but somewhat less frightening. He pulled two coffee mugs down off the shelf, blew the dust out of them and then poured the coffee. He handed one to Molly and took the other mug with him to the desk on the other side of the room.

Molly pulled a stool up in front of him and blew cool air onto the hot coffee. She waited until Matt had taken a draw of his coffee until she spoke again.

"Matt. Are you telling me that you didn't find Sierra?"

"Yeah! That's exactly what I'm telling you. I don't know what happened to her."

They had ridden out of town early Tuesday morning. At first Smitty Cohan thought for sure he had located the print of Sierra's horse. They went just a short distance before he realized that it suddenly disappeared. Figuring she had cut off the trail, they had spent a lot of time looking for more tracks. They never found any. Deciding that she may have moved from the trail onto the grassy area, they kept going east. They had no idea why would she leave town in an easterly direction and then suddenly turn in a different direction. There was only one trail at this point. They rode for hours and found nothing. At nightfall they bedded down close to the river and decided to leave early the next morning and just keep riding east. Sometime around noon the next day they passed a couple of cowhands that were heading for Overton. They hadn't seen any rider going in the opposite direction. They said they had been riding for four days. Matt hated to give up the search, but knew it wouldn't be a reasonable thing to keep doing. Smitty suggested that maybe we should criss-cross the trail on the way home and maybe we could find something that way. So that's what they had done. It had taken lots longer to get home that way, but they had given it every attempt to find her tracks.

"I just don't know what to think Molly. After we lost the trail on that first morning, it was like she just went up in smoke. I don't suppose that you have heard anything from her have you?"

"Not a thing Matt. I'm beginning to get scared about this. No one just totally disappears without a trace."

"Especially since she didn't let either one of us know that she was leaving. Something is very wrong, but I don't know what. I guess I'll ask around town some more and see if I can find out anything. Then I'm going to ride to all the neighboring farms and ranches and see if anyone there has seen her."

"I'll keep my eyes and ears open when a new customer comes into the saloon. You never know who might have run into her someplace."

"Meantime, let's both keep watch on her shop. See if we see any activity around there. If she is close by, she might come in and get some of her clothes. But dammit! Where is she? I thought she and I had something special going on. We didn't know each other for too long, but we just seemed to fit together. I think I was falling for her."

"I figured that Matt. I'm sure that she felt the same way about you. I could just tell by the way she looked at you when you didn't know she was looking. And it's the same thing for me. She and I had become good friends. We really enjoyed each others company. You know being in the business that I'm in, I don't make too many 'girl friends'. But this time I felt a real connection with her. It didn't matter a wit that I ran the town saloon. She was – jeepers! I mean she is someone special.

"Well, I'll spend today checking out the town. I also want to check out about that stranger that was at the dance last Saturday. I have this creepy feeling that he might have had something to do with Sierra's disappearance. She sure seemed mighty upset after he talked to her. See what you can find out too Molly."

"Consider it done Matt."

* * * *

Walking around town Matt questioned everyone he saw. No one had seen Sierra since Saturday night. The last time she was seen was Sunday morning at the livery stable. Matt decided to go back and talk to Gabe. Maybe he had forgotten to tell me something she said.

"Gabe, go over your conversation with Sierra once more will you? I keep feeling that her visit here is the key to the whole mystery. You said she came here early Sunday morning. What time was it?"

"Gosh Matt! I wasn't even out of bed when she knocked on the door. Guess she walked down from her shop. But then it isn't very far for her to walk. It was just barely daylight. I guess that it would be around five or six. She didn't seem her usual smiling self. She was dressed for riding. When she asked me about renting a horse, I asked her if she had ridden before and she told me she had, but it had been several years ago. She said that she had better have a horse that wouldn't give her any trouble. I brought out Stormy and told her not to judge him by his name. She said she only needed him until sometime in the afternoon. She wanted to pay me up front, but I told her to wait until she brought him back. Said I wasn't worried about getting my money. After all, I knew where to find her if she cheats me. Ironic ain't it? I really don't know where to find her. That's all I remember Matt. If I knew anything more I would tell you."

"I know you would Gabe. Thanks for your help. I don't know what else to do. I've checked all around town and nobody knows where she went. Guess I'll just have to wait it out. Unless... Just had a thought Gabe, I'll see you later."

Matt walked back to the Sheriff's office and unhitched the reins of his horse from the rail. His mind was racing. "I wonder if she might have gone out to the old farm? Maybe she rode east just to be alone, and then decided to take a ride out to the farm for the day, liked it so much she stayed. It's worth a try. Sitting around here doing nothing is driving me crazy."

He pulled on the reins and his horse seemed to feel the urgency. He wheeled around and with the silent command from Matt, he was flying. They covered ground quickly, the man and the animal he was astride. The ride seemed to take longer than it should have done, but they covered it as if they had wings. Matt couldn't help but feel that this was a last resort as far as finding Sierra goes. He didn't have a clue as to what else he would do if she wasn't at the farm. Finally, the entrance to the farm came into view. The closer Matt got, the more his heart sank. No horse outside the house. Maybe it's in the old barn. No, she knew that the barn was ready to fall down. She wouldn't put the horse in harm's way. He glanced around at the pasture, hoping to see the horse grazing there. It was empty, except for the tall waving weeds that had taken it over. He pulled up to the house and jumped off his horse.

"Sierra! Sierra, are you here?"

His question was answered with an echo from the empty building.

"Sierra! Answer me if you're here. Dammit! Where are you?"

He walked into the front room of the house and looked about. Someone had been here. There were foot prints in the dust on the floor. They looked pretty big to be Sierra's though. Wait! Over here, that looks like a small woman's boot print. The dust on the table had been disturbed. There was a coffee mug on it that wasn't there the last time he came out here. The center of the room had the look of a lot of activity. Hardly any dust. An old pot was on the stove and looked as if something had been cooked in it and never washed. He didn't remember it being there last time he was here with Sierra. Slowly he glanced around the room and found several things out of place. The old rocker was in front

117

of the stove. As if someone had had a fire and had sat in front of it. Matt carefully walked over to the steps that led up to the attic bedroom. Drawing his gun, he slowly climbed the steps. Every bone in his body was alert for danger that could be hiding in the attic. When his eyes could see over the edge of the landing he could tell that no one was there. Re-holstering his gun, he looked around. The bed was a total mess. All the old cobwebs that had been there before were now gone. It looked like someone had slept there. What was that, attached to the bedpost? Straps? What in the world. Someone was tied up to the top of the bed. A bowl of food set on the table next to the bed. Looks like whoever's it was, hadn't eaten any of it. It had to be only a couple of days old. It hadn't spoiled. What went on in this house? There had to be at least two people involved. One was tied up and the other did the cooking. He could only see the bigger of the foot prints up here on the floor, so I guess that a man had a woman held here. He cooked for her. Who were they? How long were they here? When did they leave?

"Oh my god! Could the woman have been Sierra? It seems to fit the pattern."

Matt walked down the steps and out onto the porch. Looking around the back of the house he discovered the wheel marks of a wagon. Tracks told him that there had been two horses tied up to the fence around the barn and one of them had a nick out of a shoe. Just like Gabe had described. Sierra's horse! Following the tracks, backward, he realized that the wagon had come from the direction of town. He couldn't decipher if the horse with one rider had arrived ahead of the wagon, or if the wagon had come first. He returned to the barn area and located the tracks of the wagon leaving the farm. It looked as if the single horse was tied to the back of the wagon.

Deciding to follow the tracks, Matt set out at a slow pace. He didn't want to lose the trail. A gnawing suspicion crept into his whole being. Could it have been Sierra that was tied to the bed? That would explain her disappearance. But why… ? He'd get an answer just as soon as he found that wagon. "Careful", he told himself. "Don't do anything rash. If the man is kidnapping Sierra he'll fight to keep her. Probably even kill. I have to remember, that she is in jeopardy."

By the looks of the tracks, they could be one maybe even two days ahead of him. He was prepared to follow as long as it took. He knew that if anything came up in Wild River Junction when he was away, that Jethro could handle it. The wagon was leading as if going back into town when the tracks took a swing toward the north, across a grassy section of land. He followed it with caution.

Several hours had passed since he had started tracking. The light was fading fast and he knew he would have to spend the night out under the stars again. He always carried a supply of beef jerky with him in his saddle bags and a canteen of water hanging from his saddle horn. He never knew when he would be gone for long periods of time if he was tracking a wanted man. The dark night closed in around him and he settled into his blanket. He had tied his horse near by and it would let him know if anyone was around. Finding sleep was hard. Not only because of the chill in the night or the hardness of the ground, but the pictures that kept running through his mind. He didn't want to believe that it was Sierra that had been in the house, but he just couldn't get it out of his mind.

"Just as soon as dawn breaks, I'm out of here. I'll follow that wagon until I catch up with the driver. Then I'll get my answers. If I'm lucky, I should catch up by tomorrow afternoon, late."

Chapter 17

The sun was beginning to rise over the top of the distant hills when Matt awoke. He had slept longer than he had meant to, but then he hadn't slept very well all night. It must have been just about an hour ago that he fell into a deep sleep. He stretched his long body and began to roll up his blanket. His faithful steed was still close by and enjoying the sweet new grass that was growing beside the stream. After tying the blanket to his saddle Matt fished around in the saddle bags for another piece of jerky. He put it into a pocket of his jacket for later on. Grabbing the horn of his saddle he pulled himself up onto the horse. He leaned over and untied the reins from the branch of the tree. Nudging the horse with his knees, they took of at a slow pace, following the wagon tracks.

With the brisk morning nibbling at his nose, Matt pushed on with a new resolve. No matter how far he had to go, he was going to follow them to the end. And suddenly there it was in the distance.

He couldn't believe that he had caught up with them already. The wagon and two horses were out in the open. No one seemed to be around. The horse harnessed to the wagon had his head down and was eating. At the back was another horse, tethered to the back of the wagon. Strange! No one anywhere! Matt approached the rig cautiously. Just beyond the wagon there was a water supply tower and it was right next to railroad tracks.

"Holy shit! They took the train from here. I wonder which direction they were headed. Damn! I'll never find out what happened at the house now."

Looking the wagon over, Matt climbed on top. He noticed a ribbon lying on the floor. This could only have come from a woman, he thought. Did Sierra have a ribbon like this? It's hard to say. All ribbons look alike to a man. Maybe Molly will know. Matt reached over to his horse and tied it to the other corner of the wagon. Then he began the long trip back to Wild River Junction. Again he had failed to get any answers. Again he felt that he had failed Sierra. That is, if the woman was Sierra. He figured that he would check out the train schedule once he reached town and maybe he could get some idea as to where they had gone. Of course, he wasn't exactly sure what day they had got on the train. It had to have been within the past two days.

With his spirit depleted. Matt drove the wagon all the way back to Wild River Junction without stopping. Dog tired and a heavy heart gave him the strength to continue on late into the night. The next morning, with the sun streaming down on a fatigued human, Matt pulled into Wild River. Before he knew it, he was surrounded by a crowd of town people.

"Did you find her Sheriff?"

"Where did you get the wagon Sheriff?"

It took all the strength that Matt had to climb down from the wagon at the livery stable. Gabe met him outside, and exclaimed that the horse tied to the back of the wagon was the one that Sierra has borrowed. Well, at least Matt now knew that it must have been Sierra that was in the house and the one that was put on board the train.

"Gabe, take care of my horse for me will you. He's mighty tired and needs to be rubbed down. Give him an extra portion of oats too."

"Where'd you find them Matt?"

"They were about twenty miles out of town. Found them over by the train tracks right where the water tower is. Figured that the minute the train stopped for water, whoever had left them climbed on board. I don't know which direction they were going though, or even when they did it. It looks like Sierra was being held against her will and was forced to go with whoever he is. Do you recognize the wagon Gabe?"

"Something about it seems familiar. Let me think on it for a while. Why don't you go to the office and sleep for a while?"

"Oh yes, and have Molly breaking down my door again. No. I'm going to tell Molly what happened. She isn't going to be any happier than I am. Thanks Gabe. Will you put the wagon out back until I decide what to do with it?"

Word had spread as quickly as a prairie fire. Before Matt had turned the corner of the street he saw Molly running down to meet him.

"Where in the hell have you been. You leave town and don't say a word. I didn't know what to think. I thought we were in this together. Why did you just go off on your own and not tell me where you were going?"

"Sorry Molly. Say, can we talk over a tall glass of beer? I'm mighty tired and thirsty?"

They made their way back into the saloon and Matt sat down at one of the tables. He wanted to make sure that no one overheard what he was about to tell Molly.

"I rode out to the old farm, Moll. You know, Sierra and I had gone out there a while ago. I got to wondering if maybe she had gone back out there for some reason. Well, I was right. I firmly believe that she was at the farm and that she met up with some man there. I found signs of a struggle in the house, even found some old rope tied around the bedpost. It looks as if she was tied up. Old Gabe's horse had been around the back of the house along with a horse and wagon. I don't know how long they had stayed at the house or even how close I was to finding them. I followed the wagon tracks. I had to go slow so that I wouldn't lose the tracks. When night came I camped out and started out early the next morning. I hadn't been going long at all when I spied the wagon and the two horses. They had been left right next to the water tower by the train tracks. It looks as if they both got on the train when it stopped for water. I'm going to check with Paul at the station and see when the next train comes in. Maybe someone on that train could have seen Sierra when she got on and they could tell me what direction they were headed. Might even know what town they got off. It's a long shot, but it's worth a try. But one thing I'm sure of Moll, Sierra didn't leave of her own free will."

"It sure sounds like it Matt. But if she was at the house, how did the man know she was there? Unless… unless she had planned to meet him there. But why would she meet someone she thought would do her harm?"

"Same questions I've been asking myself Moll. The only conclusion I can come up with is that she didn't think she would be in trouble. Damn! There are so many questions and no answers."

"Matt, how about we go down to Sierra's shop and just look through her things. I hate to do it, but then we may get some clue as to what happened, or even who the man was."

"That's a great idea Molly. Why don't you go on down and start looking while I go over to see Paul at the station. It shouldn't take me long at all. I'll come by when I'm finished."

* * * *

Everything in town was close by even the train depot. It only took Matt about 15 minutes to get there. The town had been here before the station was built. The town people had decided that they didn't want the station too close. Even though there was only one train a week that came through, they felt that they didn't need the noise that came with it. Besides, it was established that the town would grow now that the trains where so close and they would build towards the depot.

It was a pleasant drive when you had someone to meet, or someone to take to the train. The trail led down to and along side of the river. It curved along for a ways following the flowing water. Wild River Junction had received its name from this river always rushing someplace, waiting for nothing or no one. In the spring, when the waters flowed down from the hills, the river coursed its way letting everyone know with a voice that seemed to shout that it was mean and meant trouble. When the water was low in the summer time it still managed to gurgle its way along, still sending out a warning to all that it was nothing to be handled lightly. The river bed was deep enough into the gorge that it never overflowed its banks. But beautiful was the only word for it. It was mesmerizing when you sat on the bank and watched the water flow before your eyes. The leaf that had just floated from the tree and slowly fell onto the water was gathered up into the arms of the white caps and carried, fast down the roaring pull of the slight drop, into a deep pool and spun around and around in the circle of the whirlpool. It was finally pulled under and then spat out again several feet down river.

Matt rode along until he reached the wooden bridge that spanned the river. Crossing over, he heard the echo of his horse's hooves as they were placed on the wooden planks. There in the distance was the train depot, looking very lonely and empty. The only reason that Paul came out here when there were no trains scheduled, was because of the Western Union lines. Wild River didn't get too many wires, but when one came in it was usually important. The last one that Matt had received was from the Sheriff in Overton. He wanted to know if Matt had seen anything of a Brock Booker. Seemed

Mr. Booker was supposed to be heading to Wild River with a lot of cash in his pocket to buy a prize mare. No one had seen or heard from him for several weeks. Matt had wired back that no one by that name had arrived.

Paul was sitting outside the depot. He seemed oblivious to the fact that Matt had ridden up. He was sitting on a bench in front of the waiting room. His shirt was unbuttoned at the top and his tie was undone. The rhythmic lifting of his chest was barely noticeable, and the slight nasal snort coming from his mouth was a dead give away that he was sleeping.

Matt hitched up his horse and then quietly walked across the wooden platform. He sat down on the bench next to Paul and waited a moment. Then he gave a loud coughing sound. Paul bounded up off the bench as if he had been shot.

"Good grief Matt. What are you trying to do? Give me a heart attack? "

"Sorry Paul, but I got tired of sitting here waiting for you to wake up."

"How long have you been here?"

"Oh, about two hours."

"Like hell you have. I just sent a wire at 11 and its only 11:15 now."

"Well it seems like I've been sitting here for a couple of hours. Do you nap everyday at this time Paul?"

"No! I never nap. But last night I was up till late trying to convince my wife that we don't need another child. My God, we already have eleven. We have to quit some time. I never knew a woman that loved kids like Mandy does. Every time she has a new baby she says that this will be the last, but then about a year later, here we go again. I'm thinking of moving out here to the depot for good. That way I can get some sleep and also not have to worry about her getting pregnant again."

"Come on Paul, you know you don't mean that. Remember two years ago you tried to move out here? It wasn't long before you missed the loving you got from Mandy, and home you went. That was two babies ago wasn't it?"

"You would have to bring that up wouldn't you? How do some of these men get by with just one or two children? Think I'll have to talk to someone and find out how they do it."

"Paul, you know how to do it. What you want to learn is how you don't do it."

"You're real funny Matt. You're really funny. You just wait until you get married and have a slew of kids around you. That's when I'm going to be the one laughing."

"That's a deal Paul. You have my permission to laugh all you want. Now! Let's get down to business. Paul, I was following some people the other day and their trail took me to the water tower. These people got on the train there. Is there any way that I could find out which direction the train was going, and also what station they got off?"

"Well, let's see! The train crew usually stays with the train from start to finish on this route. The earliest you could talk to anyone who would have been on the train is tomorrow. You know the train comes through here heading east every Monday, then heading west, every Thursday. Really nothing we can do until tomorrow when the east bound comes through. I'll send out a wire to tell them to stop here. Probably be around 1:00 p.m."

"Thanks Paul. That will be real helpful. I'll just be on my way and let you get back to your napping. Sweet dreams."

"Oh some day, I'm going to be the one laughing buddy. See you tomorrow."

* * * *

As Matt got down from his horse in front of Sierra's Finery, he felt a jab in his heart. His feelings for her had gone deeper than even he realized. When he was with her last Saturday he knew that he was falling for her, but now he realized that it had already happened. How could it be? He hadn't known her for very long. He had seen her around town from time to time but nothing about her made his heart pound. Then when they met and spent some time together it was a different story. Not love at first sight, but darned near.

"Molly? Are you still here?" Matt called as he entered the door. The shop seemed cold without Sierra's laugher and presence.

"Back here Matt. I've found a couple of things that might help. Here, read this letter. It's from back east. A place called Stonehigh, Vermont. The name on the letter is Arletta Daniels. She talks about a little girl by the name of Annie. It tells all that the girl says and does. I don't get it!"

"Sounds kind' a like a report. Like Sarah would be interested in this child. Hey! Molly you don't suppose that she is Sierra's daughter? Sierra never mentioned having a child, but then she hasn't really talked about her past. Maybe she had to leave town to go and get her kid."

"I don't think so Matt. It could possibly be her child, but Sierra would never have gone on a long trip like that and not taken her clothes with her. Besides, you seemed to believe that she was taken by force from your farm house."

"Yeah, you're right Molly. This whole thing is a lot deeper than just hiding a child from us. What else did you find?"

"Something strange! I found your old family bible. It's on the table next to her bed. What was she doing with it here?"

"What! Let me see it. Your right, it's the bible that mom and pop kept in the farm house. I remember the day that they added my name to the family section. Here it is, right here. That's funny. When Sierra and I went out to the farm a couple of weeks ago I couldn't find the bible. I was really upset about someone stealing it. Why in God's name would she have taken it and not told me about it? She must have taken it before she and I went out there. This situation seems to get stranger all the time. There's a big chunk of her life that needs a lot of explaining."

"Any luck out at the depot?"

"Naw. Paul says the train will be coming through to-morrow about 1:00 p.m. He's sending a wire to have the train stop at the station. Maybe I'll get some kind of news from the conductor. I don't know where else to look. This is the only clue that I have."

Molly and Matt took one last long look around the rooms and decided there was nothing else to find. If Sierra had left on her own volition then why hadn't they heard from her? If she had been forced to leave, there was really nothing more that could be done. The only chance was to get some information from the train workers tomorrow. After that, who knows?

* * * *

The smoke was curling upward as the engine pulled around the bend. Hope was high for Matt and it seemed to take forever for the train to arrive at the station and pull to a stop.

The conductor jumped off the train before it came to a halt, and he placed a stool on the platform beside the doorway. Yelling loudly he announced to the departing passengers that this was only a very short stop and that anyone not returning promptly to the train when the whistle blew, would be left at the station.

"Good afternoon Abe. Hey you're almost on time. Only one hour and five minutes late." Paul teased the tall man in the conductor uniform.

"It could have been worse. We had to remove a dead horse from the tracks just out of Overton. No too many of the passengers wanted to help pull the animal off to the side. Pretty damned heavy I'll tell you. Poor animal! Not sure how he died. First one I've seen in several years. Now Paul, where is this passenger you wired us to pick up?"

"No Abe. I didn't wire you to pick up a passenger. I just said to be sure to stop at the station today."

"What in the hell is that all about?" Abe asked irritably. To him the only reason to stop the train was to either pick up or de-embark passengers. Everything else was a waste of time.

"Abe, this is our Sheriff Matt Rathburn. He has some questions that he needs to ask you regarding some passengers that got on the train. He'll tell you all about it. It's very important. Why don't you both come into the office and have a cup on coffee?"

"I don't have time for coffee Paul. You already informed me that I was late. I don't intend to be much later. Alright Sheriff, what is this all about?"

"I trailed some people last Tuesday and they seemed to have got on the train at the water tower east of town. I was wondering if you remember a man and a woman getting on at that point?"

"Sure! I remember them. He seemed pretty rough with her. He paid fares to Overton. I asked him what he was going to do about the horses and wagon that he left beside the tracks. He told me to mind my own business. When we reached Overton, they got off the train and went into the depot. It was my short trip that time and I finished up there. Pretty soon I saw them both getting back onto the train. I asked the station master where they were going. He said that they hadn't said anything. Just mulled around the station and then when the whistle blew, he grabbed her by the wrist and literally pulled her back onto the train. We figured that he purchased more tickets on the train after it pulled out. That's all I can tell you."

"Do you think the conductor that took over for you that day from Overton would be able to remember them?"

"I doubt it. There was a crowd of people that got on the train. Overton is a pretty busy depot for passengers, both coming and going. I can talk to him next time I see him, if you like? But I can't promise it will come to anything. If he can remember anything I'll send a message on the next train coming through and let Paul know."

"I would appreciate that Abe. It's very important. I have to find out where they went. Thanks for taking the time to talk to me."

Abe turned around and the sound of his shrill whistle cut through the air. He returned to the train doorway just as the train's loud steam whistle sounded. Passengers that had been standing around or walking to stretch their legs headed for the train. In no time at all the passengers were safely installed inside the cars and the train began to chug – chug as the engine got its steam up and slowly slipped out of the depot. Watching it as it disappeared out of sight, Matt felt a sinking feeling in his stomach. "How much further down the line did they travel? Where did they get off?" His mind was racing. How is it that every lead keeps leading to nowhere? Maybe the man knew that someone would come looking for them. He seemed to be covering their tracks. "There has got to be something that I can do. Each day puts her in more danger. I'll wait until the next train comes through and see if Abe might have been able to find out anything."

Telling Molly the disappointing news was going to be hard. She was hoping, as was he, that the conductor would be able to give them a lead. "Poor Molly, she is as baffled as

I am. Who is Annie? And why was my bible in her bedroom? I'll get some answers somehow. Molly hears lots of stories from her customers. Maybe one of them will have come upon Sierra. Wishful thinking! You bet. But I will never give up trying to figure this out".

Chapter 18

"When do we leave for Overton?" This was the first thing that Molly stated after Matt told her about his talk with Abe. It came as a surprise that she wanted to be included in the search, but then when you think about it, it was a Molly thing.

"I don't think you should go Molly. It's a couple of days hard riding on a horse, longer if we take a buggy. I haven't made up my mind yet if we should wait for the next train to get the information or go over myself."

"If we wait for the train, that's another four days. I'm all for going to Overton and if we get any leads there we can follow them up. I just can't sit here and wait any longer. I want to be doing something to help. We'll take our horses. I'm not asking you Matt, I'm letting you know that I'm going, with or without you."

"What if she comes back and needs you, then what?"

"If she comes back she'll just have to survive without me. But you and I know she isn't going to come back on her own Matt. This poor kid is in trouble and we have to do whatever we feel is right. I'm going upstairs and throw a couple of things in my satchel. Let's meet down here in one hour. That will give me time to make arrangements with Boots about closing at night. Now go, get your house in order too."

"Molly, you're a stubborn old girl, but I love you anyway. See you in one hour. I'll get Gabe to saddle your horse and I'll grab some food for us. We'll have to camp out over night so be sure to bring a blanket with you and anything else you think you might need to survive the wilderness. You better bring your rifle along too."

Matt would have felt better if he could have made this trip by himself, but he also knew that if he didn't take Molly along with him, she would only be following him. He would rather have her where he could watch her. Not that Molly needed protecting. She had taken many a cowpoke to task when they became rowdy in her saloon. She knew how to use that rifle too. Rumor has it that she was able to shoot before she could even lift the rifle.

One hour later Matt rode up to the door of the saloon with Molly's horse in tow. Both of their saddle bags were jammed full of the things they would need to keep them going. Water canteens hung around the saddle horn. Molly walked through the doors and slung her valise on the back of her horse and tied it down. She pulled a bottle of scotch from the folds of her dress and put it into her saddle bag.

"What's that for Moll, snake bite?"

"You bet your sweet ass it is."

Putting her foot into the stirrup, Molly pulled herself up onto the saddle and threw her leg over the top. She was wearing a pair of saddle pants that she had bought from Sierra's Finery. Sierra had made her think that she just couldn't live without them as an addition to her wardrobe. She never dreamt that she would be wearing them to search for her friend. She was all set to be as comfortable on this trip as she could be. She didn't want to be a burden to Matt. She knew that he would rather she stayed here, but she just couldn't.

Boots walked out onto the wooden sidewalk and watched as the two friends rode away. He knew that this trip was important to Molly and anything important to her was important to him. Silently he wished them good luck, and he then turned around and went back inside. He knew that Molly would never worry about the place while she was gone. She trusted him completely. He had never given her any reason not to in all the time that they had known each other.

* * * *

As he walked back into the saloon Boots couldn't help but remember what had brought him to the Wild River Saloon.

Boots had been in bad shape the first time he came into Wild River Junction. He was only 36 years old, but looked much older. Life for the past 10 years hadn't been good to him.

He had finally laid old devil alcohol in the dirt and beat him. It had been a fight for his life and it had taken its toll.

Always fresh in his mind was the terrible day when those lousy bastards had ridden onto his farm. They had found his wife alone. He had gone on a hunting trip with Zack his eldest son and they had ridden out for two days. They had slept under the stars that first night and everything seemed to be as God had planned it. Not a cloud in the sky and the stars shone so bright that you could see everything in the heavens. He and Zack had always been close and this hunting trip seemed to bring them even closer. There was some good natured teasing about my cooking not being anywhere near as good as moms and I had told him that on the return trip he could do the cooking. It didn't seem to scare him too much.

Game had been so plentiful that they had been able to cut the trip short. Anxious to get home to see his lovely Charity and their two year old baby boy, John, the two hunters had ridden all night on the return trip. Neither one of them could wait to brag about the fine assortment of game that they had been able to bring back home. This was Zack's first hunting trip and he was so proud. He had been able to hold up his end of the hunt and Boots had realized that he was going to be a good hunter when he got older. Guess all 10 year olds look forward to time with their dads. Just the two 'men' alone together, sharing a world of new experiences.

As they came up over the hill they looked down at the farm house. Boots was so proud of their home. A lot of hard work had gone into it, but the end result was rewarding. It didn't seem possible that they had been living here for over ten years. Charity had been a big help. Even though she was slightly built she was able to help lift some of the heavy timber. Just looking at her you would have thought that she was only capable of sitting with a delicate cup of tea in her hands.

The house was surrounded by a white picket fence. Charity had requested this for her birthday. She'd had all three of us out there painting it. Even little John. She said it was never too early for a child to learn. We all laughed when he fell into the bucket of white wash and came out covered. She never asked for much and I just couldn't refuse her this request.

Boots noticed that the place looked deserted. Usually the three dogs were running all over the place chasing the chickens. This was their favorite sport. Of course the chickens were faster than the dogs and he swore that they deliberately teased the dogs into the chase.

But Boots couldn't see any dogs or chickens. Just an eerie calm enveloped the place. Not a breeze stirred. Even the tall grass stood up tall and never wavered. He felt... an urgency. He had to get to the house fast and he spurred his horse forward. The pack mule he was leading objected and Boots gave the rope to Zach to hold. As he reached the front door he noticed that it was wide open. Charity would never have let that happen. She was always afraid of what might crawl into the house and surprise her. He jumped from his saddle and ran through the door.

He had found her on the floor beside the fireplace. Her skirts had been pulled up around her neck and she was bare from the waist down. Blood covered her legs and her eyes held no life at all. He scrambled to cover her nakedness before Zack walked into the room and then he cradled her in his arms. She was gone. Dead! Dear God, she had been so violently assaulted but why? Who? Zack came running into the room and cried out in that half man half boy voice.

"Dad, what happened?"

"I don't know son. I just don't know."

"Dad, where's John?"

Boots scrambled to his feet and started searching the cabin. He and Zack called out to John. There was no response. They ran outside and yelled as loud as they could.

"John! John where are you? This is daddy, come here this minute. I need to find you."

Nothing but the silence of the plains echoed back. They spent hours searching the farm. They looked in the barn, the chicken house, the pig sty, down the well; they even rode out for several miles and looked. There was no sign of John.

Boots couldn't believe that his life had taken such a tragic turn in just a few days. He had been gone for just three days. Oh, my dear sweet Charity. She must have been so terrified.

"Dad, don't you think we should go into town and tell the Sheriff?"

"Yeah Zack. I have to tell him about your mom, but before we bury her we must find little John. Maybe someone in town knows what happened and who was involved. Could be someone has him. Hurry, we have to find John. Let's put

your mom up on the bed and cover her. We'll bury her this evening when we get back."

The ride into town had taken them a little over an hour. They traveled slowly so that they wouldn't miss any trace of John. They scoured the scenery as they went in hopes of seeing him.

No one in town knew anything about the attack. No strangers had been seen in the area and worst of all they still couldn't find out what had happened to young John. It had been suggested that maybe whoever had killed Charity had taken John. Boots shuddered at this suggestion. The sheriff assembled a posse and assured Boots that they would find some trail of the killers. He told Boots to go home in case young John came back and he would let Boots know if they found out anything.

As the two of them made they way back to the farm, facing the dreaded chore of burying their beloved wife and mother, Boots noticed something strange in the distance. Some old turkey buzzards were circling up high and then making a dive down to just below the ridge. Boots rode over to the area and found young John. He had been mauled to death by one of the predators that lived here on the land. It was probably a mountain lion. John had evidently walked out of the cabin when he realized that his mother wouldn't wake up and he had crossed the prairie. He must have got lost and couldn't find his way back to the house.

So Boots and Zack had buried two bodies that evening. After the grueling deed was done, Boots grabbed his hidden bottle from inside the well, and walked out onto the prairie.

He couldn't remember much about the following 8 years. It was all a blur of hurt and pain and oblivion.

He woke up one morning and found himself sleeping under the steps that lead up into a saloon. He was filthy, and smelled terrible. He had such a bad thirst that his belly burned inside him. He crawled out from under the steps and walked into the saloon. The bartender came around the end of the bar and grabbed Boots by the neck and pushed him outside and down the steps.

"Stay out of here you drunken bum. You stink too bad to be around people. Don't ever come in here again. No wonder that poor boy of yours rode out of town with those drifters. You aren't a man. You're a horror show."

Boots couldn't comprehend what he had just heard.

"What's the matter with you man? I'm not a smelly bum. I'm a man who has a family and a nice farm. What's he talking about? What's he mean that my son went off with some drifters? Is he talking about Zack? Couldn't be John, he's still a baby."

It was at this moment that all the hurt and pain came rushing back. His Charity was gone, his baby boy was gone. How long had it been? He tried to figure it out, but his brains were so scrambled and he needed a drink so bad. The last thing he remembered was walking away from two freshly dug graves and reaching for the secret bottle that he kept hidden from Charity. Where had he been since then? How long had he been drinking? He picked himself up off the street and started walking.

"I've got to find out the answer to my questions. Who would know? Maybe the Sheriff?"

As he walked he stumbled and fell. Tears filled his eyes and he screamed out loud with the frustration of it all.

A gentle hand touched his shoulder and helped him to his feet and set him down on the wooden sidewalk.

"Are you alright?"

"I don't know. I'm not sure who I am or where I am. I need some answers and no one will help me."

"Why don't you come with me and I'll get Doc to take a look at you."

"Who are you?"

"They call me Molly."

"Why are you bothering with a dirty smelly object like me?"

"You're not an object, you're a human being. We should all help each other."

Looking back over the years, Boots remembered the struggle he went through to survive. He never could have done it without Molly's help. It took time, but he was able to straighten himself out and rediscover life.

After several years of searching he finally found Zack and was able to contact him. They had written back and forth for about a year now. Someday they would meet again. This was a dream that Boots had, besides the dream that Molly would let him be more than a friend to her.

Chapter 19

There wasn't an inch that wasn't covered in dust. It itched. It stuck to her body where she had sweated. Her eyes felt as if they were on fire from the dry burning sensation. And her hair! No matter how she had covered it, it was stiff, gritty and looked like she had a pile of straw on her head. And sleeping on the ground at night didn't help the situation either. You could search the ground for rocks under your blanket but you never seemed to get them all. You lay down and the minute you change positions, there it was, you found another one. Aches and pains were just a part of the joy of traveling.

Molly didn't ride horses too often. She was always happy and content to stay in her saloon, or take a walk through town. Once in a while she would rent a buggy and go out for a ride. But climbing up on a horse was something that never did work for her. She was a little afraid of the big animals she tried to ride and never trusted that they would take directions from her. She always seemed to end up with a horse that either didn't want to go the same way she did, or else it wanted to gallop everywhere. One time she had been riding and the horse ran up to the nearest fence and rubbed against it trying to get her off the saddle. She knew when she and Matt set out on their trip that it would be a hard journey for her. She had been right. It had been. But to her credit she hadn't complained. It was a necessary evil that she'd had to endure.

They had been gone for six days. Two days to Overton, two days there and two days back. The feel of her body submerged in the hot soapy water in her tub had been the dream that had kept her going for the past twenty four hours. Finally, it was a reality. Here she was, at home in her place, in her tub and the peace and tranquility filled her every nerve ending. Every aching muscle cried out in thanks for the heat. She thought about the trip. How could anyone completely disappear without a trace? No one in Overton had seen Sierra. The train conductor remembered that a man and woman had got on the train at the watering spot, but after that, he couldn't remember seeing them again. He said that they must have bought a ticket from him, but he just couldn't remember. It seems that at that specific time there had been a bad fight on the train between two wranglers. It had caused quite a ruckus and several of the passengers had been injured. So, anything else was completely forgotten. He had said that he was sorry. He wasn't anywhere near as sorry as Matt and Molly were. They had spent two days walking into each and every hotel, shop and even the saloons in town. The livery man said that he hadn't rented or sold any horses or buggies during that time. How can two grown people just disappear like a puff of smoke?

The knock on the door brought Molly back to the real world.

"Molly, its Boots. I've got another bucket of hot water for you and also a nice big glass of something warm. I'll leave it out here in the hall."

"For heaven's sake Boots, we've been around each other long enough to forget about modesty. The door is unlocked. Just bring in the hot water and the drink. I can use each of them. Besides, I put enough salts into this tub to make big bubbles. You can only see my eyes and my toes."

"I just didn't want to barge in. I knew you were in the tub. I remember once before, many years ago, I caught you in the tub and you almost shot me. If I had waited another two seconds I believe you would have. It was a good thing that your hand was wet and slippery. You might have had another bartender by now if that gun hadn't slipped."

"Yes, but at that time I was having trouble with old Mac. I really thought it was his voice I heard not yours. Wow! How close was that one?"

Boots walked across the floor of the bathing room and lifted the bucket into the air. Gently he poured the hot water into the tub. She looked like an angel to him. The water made the bubbles rise up and the white foam enveloped Molly. Her black hair was framed with the white of the bubbles and it took all the strength he had to not grab her and pull her to him. He knew that if he did it would put an end to their long friendship. Molly didn't mess around with anyone who worked for her. In fact, Molly didn't mess around with many people at all. She always kept her dignity and anytime she had a special relationship she was very discreet. If her special partner didn't want to go along with this, she didn't hesitate, she dumped him. What strength she had. She would sure make some lucky man a good wife. He had often wondered if Molly had a thing for Matt, but he knew that Matt was much too young for Molly. They had also been friends for many years. Besides, Matt had taken up with Sierra. He could tell by looking at Matt when Sierra was around that she meant an awful lot to him. Boots remembered that the first time he realized this he was overcome with joy. He had always thought that there was always that chance that would bring Matt and Molly together romantically.

"Boots, you're gonna make that water cold. Pour it in quickly, damn it. Sit down over there and tell me anything exciting that happened while I was gone. Heaven knows that I don't have anything exciting to tell you. She just disappeared. Gone! No one has seen or heard of her. I just don't know what to think. We've tried everything we can think of to find her. I am really afraid of what might have happened to her. I just have to keep thinking that she is alive and has one great reason for her leaving town and not telling us. If she does show up and doesn't have a really great excuse, I might kill her myself for what she has put me and Matt through."

"Now Molly, you know you don't mean that. You wouldn't hurt a flea. I've seen enough people give you good reason to get violent but you just kept your cool. You always won in the end."

"Yeah? Oh well, tell me about the saloon. Were you busy? Many cow pokes come into town aching to part with their wages? If you did real good, maybe I'll sell you half the saloon one day. I'm not getting any younger and I think it's time I took a partner. What do you think about that Boots?"

"I can't say that I haven't thought about doing just that Molly. The only trouble is that I just don't have the cash. I've tried to save since I started working here, but it just doesn't add up very fast."

"Well I'm not talking about doing it right this minute. I'm thinking a couple of years down the road. And by the way, I've decided to reward you for your being such a good friend over these past years. How would you feel about getting a raise, and also a small percentage of what we take in at the tables? It's past time you had something good happen to you. "

"Molly! I don't know what to say. That would be great. Thanks."

"Alright, don't start blubbering. Go on downstairs and tend to the boys. I'll be down just as soon as I get dressed. Oh, and Boots, thank you for being someone I can count on."

Walking down the stairs into the saloon always gave Molly a stab of pride. It may have been just a plain ordinary saloon to some folks, but to her it was everything in the world that was good. She had worked hard enough to put together the money it had cost her. If old Smitty hadn't up and died she would never have known that he had made it good in the old mine. You would never have known it by the way he looked. She had offered him a couple of dollars one time to buy some new clothes. The ones he wore all the time were so old, dirty and ripped. But he had turned it down. No wonder he laughed so hard. You would never have thought that he had two nickels to rub together. God love him. He had put a clause in his will that she was to receive ten percent of his holdings in immediate cash. He knew what the saloon had meant to her. It turned out that what she had been able to save over the years and with Smitty's help she was able to pay cash for her establishment.

The tables were busy tonight. There must be a herd just outside of town to bring that many wranglers in. Her thoughts buzzed inside her head. I just may have to hire myself a piano player one of these days and maybe a singer too. I would like to give the boys something special when they visit here. She couldn't see Matt anywhere. He probably went into the jail house and stretched out on one of the bunks in a cell. That poor kid. He may be a grown man, but he sure was hurting inside. "Damn it Sierra! Where in the hell are you?"

She saw that Boots was in deep conversation with one of the drovers at the bar. They seemed to be discussing the best market place for the cattle. Boots knew a lot about cattle. He had worked with them for several years when he was younger. Probably several more when he had disappeared from the face of the earth. He was a good man. "Not bad looking either." Molly decided. "Now just forget about that sort of thing you dumb broad. You'll only get yourself into deep water with thoughts like that."

* * * *

Matt had walked into his office looking like an old grisly bear. He was black from the sand and he hadn't

144

shaved since they had left six days before. He knew he looked bad, but he was so tired and so discouraged. Maybe if he could get a couple of hours sleep he would feel more like getting cleaned up. The weight of the situation brought him down into the depths of despair. Not knowing what had happened to Sierra was driving him crazy. He could only imagine the worst. He questioned himself as to whether she was still alive or not. He couldn't believe that everything that he could do had been done to no avail. Guess only time will bring an answer to his questions. There again maybe not.

He laid his bone aching body down on the straw mattress in cell three. The pillow smelt like stale beer and sweat. It didn't bother him though. He was too tired to get back up. Besides, the pillows in the other cells probably were just as bad. He thought to himself, "Someday I have to put these beds outside the back and let the sun and air get to them."

And with this on his mind, he slipped into oblivion not knowing or caring what the world was up to at that particular moment. It was a restless sleep. He dreamed non sensible dreams. In one he was riding on this great big jack rabbit. It was taking him across the plains and suddenly there was water all over the place. He was swimming away from the shore leaving the rabbit behind to flail about in the water. The next one he was standing on top of a very tall building that was so small he could hardly find room to put his feet down. The wind was blowing and the building began to sway. He felt as if he would fall and the terror of it made him breathe in short bursts. Then the deep sleep took over and he found a dark peaceful place.

It must have been twelve hours later when he finally began to stir. He tasted something sour in his mouth. It was so dry. He felt that he couldn't spit if he had to. He didn't want to open his eyes. It would have been so great to just slip back into that unknown cave of darkness. Using all his might, he forced open his eyelids. He saw nothing. Maybe he was still dreaming. He thought he would just drift back down again. Then he remembered. Sierra! How can I sleep when she needs me to find her? He reached out into the dark and felt the wall by his head. He knew that if he followed this wall it would lead him to the door of the cell and then he would follow the bars over to the doorway of the office. There would be a lamp waiting there for him. He struck a match and touched it to the wick. The glow flooded the office with a pale yellow light. He looked at the clock on the office wall. "Four o'clock in the morning. What was the time we got in yesterday? I must have slept half a day. Molly will be in bed by now. Guess I'd better not wake her. Old Boots would have my hide if I did. He watches over her twenty four hours a day." This thought brought a smile to his face. "I wonder if Molly is aware that Boots is in love with her. I bet she doesn't ever give it a thought. That poor guy. Maybe I'll start putting the word in her ear. It would have to be very gently of course. If I did it too harsh she would shy away from the fact. Gently, she may think it was her idea."

He realized that at this hour there was no hope of getting either a bath and a shave or even something to eat. A cup of coffee would help fill the hole in his stomach. The old grounds in the pot had mildewed while he was away. "Damn! Why didn't I clean out the pot before we left? Because all I could think about was getting out of here that's why." The pot smelled of old burnt coffee. He didn't have any water to wash the pot out, and he didn't have any water to make coffee with. He suddenly remembered his saddle had a water bag tied to it. Now where did he leave his horse? Over at the livery I bet. "Guess I'll just walk over and find out. Well there's nothing else to do at this time of day. Of course I'll probably have to wake old Gabe up. He'll probably raise hell with me, but I know he's an early riser so maybe he won't be too mad."

Matt walked out onto the wooden planks of the sidewalk. For just one moment he allowed himself a quick glance in the direction of "Sierra's Finery". Everything was still and dark. Just behind the shop he could see the faint light of the sunrise coming up over the hills. "Maybe this will be the day that I'll find her," he announced to himself. Then he stepped off into the street and made his way across the dusty road up to the Livery. Even in the dark he could find his way. Just the smell of the horses was like a bright beacon in the night.

Chapter 20

"Molly, don't you think its time to pack up all the things at Sierra's shop? She's been gone for almost six months."

"I've been giving that some thought Matt. It seems so final, but I guess she's not coming back. Maybe I should sell some of the merchandise at a cheaper rate to the women in town. That way I shouldn't have much to pack away. Guess I'll pass the word. Next Saturday should be good. The gals should have heard about it by then. Maybe I'll put an announcement in the local paper."

"I still keep hoping that we will hear from her. Six months! She didn't really give us a chance did she? I'm just getting to the point where I don't keep checking the shop for signs of life."

"Matt, do you want to take that bible that she had in her living quarters? You said that it had belonged to your folks. I don't want anything to happen to it while I'm packing things up."

"Yeah, thanks Molly. I almost forgot about that. Let me know next time you're going into the shop and I'll come with you."

"You wanna walk over there now? I'm not busy at this moment and I want to refresh my mind as to what merchandise she has in there."

They both walked out of the smoky saloon into the evening air. It felt good to breathe deep and feel the coolness of the fresh springtime air. Days kept getting longer, had been since Christmas time. The evening dusk had settled behind the hills and just a faint stream of light could be seen, fading away with every moment that passed. The short walk was so mechanical. They could almost count the steps it took from the saloon to the door of the shop. They had done it together so many times. Each time one or the other of them felt an urge to connect with Sierra they had come to the shop. There wasn't an inch that they hadn't searched in hope of finding something to give them a clue as to where she was. This trip was the first time in a couple of weeks. They had realized last time that it was fruitless to keep searching. At last they had given up. Neither one of them wanted to be the first to give in, but together they finally decided it was over.

The echo of footsteps rang out from the wooden sidewalk just ahead. A form oozed from the darkness almost running them down. The man seemed to be in a hurry. One glance and the recognition was instant.

"Molly! Matt! Just the two I was looking for. Wow! I ain't as young as I used to be. Sprinting just a short way takes my breath away. Give me a second."

"For heaven's sake Gabe, you scared the bejesus out of me. What in the world are you so excited about?"

"Yeah Gabe, barging up to a person like that could get you shot. What's so important?"

Gabe's wheezing breath seemed labored. Finally after a couple of seconds to get his wind he was able to talk to them.

"I was mucking out the livery about half an hour ago. It's close to my supper time and I wanted to hurry up cause I was hungry. I heard a horse walking up to the front of the livery. It stopped, and in the last light of day I noticed the rider was a woman. I asked her if I could help her and she said that she wanted to rent a stall for the horse for a couple of days. As I brought the horse inside the livery I could see the rider by the lamp light. It was Sierra! Bold as day she stood there. Looking worn out and tired. She looked as if she had ridden hard for days. The horse was covered with sweat and you could tell that it had covered a lot of ground. I asked her where in the heck she had been. I told her that everyone in town had been looking for her. She just looked at me and said that she had had an emergency and had to leave town for a while. I asked her if I could do anything to help. Would she like me to look for you two, but she said that she just wanted to get some sleep and would talk to you tomorrow. Then she pulled her belongings off of the horse and walked down the street. I waited until I saw the light go on in the shop and that's when I high tailed it to find you. She looks older. She looks like she's been to hell and back."

"Gabe, are you sure?"

"Sure as I know that stable doesn't muck itself out."

"Come on Molly, let's get down there and find out what happened."

"No Matt. If she is as dog tired as Gabe says she won't be in any mood for visitors tonight. Look! There is a light on in the shop."

"Well you do what you want Molly, but I'm feeling that I am entitled to get an explanation and the sooner the better!"

"Come on Matt. Something bad has happened and we need to give her some breathing room. Now look! The light just went out. Please Matt. Wait just a couple more hours. At least we know she's home. She'll tell us in the morning after she's had good night's sleep."

"From the way she looked Matt, she is probably dead to the world by now. Molly is right. Wait."

"Just what I need is for you two to gang up on me. Alright! I'll wait until the morning. But the morning is going to come real early tomorrow. Let's go back to the saloon

Molly and buy this livery man a drink. Thanks for coming to us so fast Gabe. We really appreciate it."

The three of them walked off in silence. Playing a waiting game didn't come easy to Matt, but he would wait. Pushing the swinging doors open they entered the saloon and walked over to the bar. Boots met them with a quizzical look on his face. He sensed that something had happened. He knew if he waited long enough he would find out without him having to ask.

"Give us three whiskies Boots on the house. Get one for yourself. We're celebrating the return of the lost lamb."

"Is this the lamb that wandered away from the flock and the shepherd's went in search of?"

"Damn right Boots. Only thing is, this lamb has a name. Sierra is back from her tousle with the devil."

"Holy man! She came back? Did she say what happened? Wow! I'm sure glad to hear she's back."

Matt glanced over at Molly and with a shrug of his shoulders he downed his drink. Grabbing his hat, he turned towards the door and walked outside. It took all his self control to not go banging on the door of Sierra's shop, but he passed by it and went down the street into the Sheriff's office. This was one night he didn't want to have too much to drink. He wanted his brain clear and alert for the next day and the story he was about to hear. The bunk in cell number one had been cleaned and aired and looked mighty inviting to him. He plopped himself down hoping that he could go to sleep fast. The next day was to be a day of reckoning.

Chapter 21

Somehow the night passed. Not in a deep slumber. She was always on the verge of dropping off into that wonderful oblivion, but never quite making it. She listened to the sounds that always raise their heads in the middle of the night, sounds that are never there in the light of day. The creaking of the bed as a position is changed, the rustling of the quilts against your skin. The coolness when you stretch out onto another part of the bed that has not been warmed by your body. Everything was just another reminder that you were finally safe at home. She was afraid to really let go in case this was just a dream and she would wake up and find herself in hell once again. Tired? She was beyond tired. Every bone in her body ached. She didn't want to open her eyes just in case she wouldn't see her lovely room around her. Tired? Every inch of every part of her body was crying out for relief. It will happen, she promised herself. Tomorrow I will sleep and heal my body. But tonight I will accept whatever the Good Lord asks of me. If I can only be aware that I am home, that is all I need. "I only ask Lord that you will guide me when I have to explain to everyone what happened and where I have been. There are things that I cannot reveal. But I will try to do my best with some of the truth. I only hope that I can convince them that it is the whole story."

* * * *

There was a knock on the door to the Sheriff's office just after sunrise. Somehow, Matt had managed to fall asleep and was astounded when he realized that someone was trying to wake him up. He quickly made his way to the office and opened the door. He was surprised to see young Pat Grady standing there.

"Sorry to wake you up so early Sheriff, but Miss Sierra asked me to bring this note to you right away. I was on my way to work and was surprised when I saw a light on in her shop. She asked me if I had time to do her a favor, and of course I said yes. I have to take a note over to the saloon too for Miss Molly. You reckon she will be awake? I don't rightly know what I'll do if the saloon is locked up tight. Anyway, here's your note."

"Thanks Pat. If it would be of any help, I could take Miss Molly's note over to her place for you. I know you have to get to work."

"Oh, that would be great. Thanks Sheriff."

Pat pushed two notes into Matt's hand and made a bee line for the street. He worked for Gabe in the livery every once in a while and everyone knew that Gabe was a stickler for his helpers being on time.

Matt looked at the paper in his hand. He recognized the writing and spent a few seconds realizing suddenly that he was holding his breath. The note was sealed with a wax imprint of a flower and Matt pulled at it carefully.

"Dear Matt; I know that I have a lot to explain, and I will. I will tell you everything. I decided that I might just as well tell my story one time, so I am asking you and Molly to have breakfast with me in the saloon at nine. I am truly sorry for everything. Sierra."

He read the note over several times. It was very short. It was to the point. "Guess I'll just have to wait for the explanation. I'd better get over to Molly's and let her know."

Somehow the night had passed and this new day was about to begin. A new day and he had this feeling of being whole again. That little piece of his life wasn't missing today. Sierra was home. For how long was anyone's guess. When you have deep feelings for someone and they do something that totally tears you apart it leaves a very bitter taste in your mouth. Building trust and love takes time. Getting back that trust when it has been shattered takes a long long time. You don't *give* your trust. It must be earned. Matt knew that he loved Sierra, but after her disappearance he wondered if he could trust her again.

Boots was sweeping the sidewalk when Matt walked up to the saloon.

"Don't you ever sleep Boots?"

"Hell, I can sleep when I'm dead. Don't want to waste any precious time."

"Will you give Molly a note for me? It seems that our lost lamb requests our presence at breakfast this morning. Tell Moll she has a couple of hours before we meet. I'm going to walk over to Doc's house and check up on a couple of things. Tell her I'll be back before nine."

"Sure thing Matt. I can't wait to hear the explanation. I'll arrange a table in the far corner for you guys to sit at. You should have some privacy there."

It only took Molly an hour to get herself up and dressed. Looking in the mirror, she once again noticed that it was her mom looking back at her. "Molly old girl, where are you? The only person I see now is someone that has been dead and gone for a long time. Sure wish I could find that sweet young thing that used to look back at me. She must have found a better life for herself. Somewhere down the road with that handsome young prince. Well, good for you I say. Sure wish it could have been me. Well, I guess it's about time for me to hightail it downstairs and get things set up for the meeting. I hope that Matt doesn't blow his top if her

154

reasoning isn't to his liking. I know that I just can't for the life of me imagine what could have caused her to go off and not leave any word. Oh well! We'll know soon enough I guess."

As Molly walked down the stairs she looked around for her bartender. Seeing him over in the corner of the saloon she noticed that his black hair was starting to get a little silver mixed in with it. She also realized that she was always happy to see him.

"Hey Boots! Have the cook fix some of those good biscuits and gravy. Good thick slabs of ham and plenty of eggs. Tell her to keep the coffee coming and I want it hot at all times. None of that warmed up crap either. Fresh brewed. This is a special event and I want everything to go well. Just imagine! Our Sierra is home again. That little shit. Hope I don't throttle her before she has a chance to explain."

"Now Molly just take a deep breath and relax. She'll tell you everything. Then, later on, you had better tell me everything. I'm as anxious as you and Matt are. Molly you want me to close up the café until you are done talking?"

"Better not Boots. Too many of the townspeople want an early breakfast. We can't afford to run off any of our customers. Thanks anyway. I think that table you picked out will be just fine. You are really a big help to me Boots. I really appreciate all that you do. Now, I think I'll just grab myself a mug of coffee and go sit and wait for the show. It should be almost time. Well, here is our illustrious Sheriff now. Grab another mug of coffee Matt and come sit with me at the table. And wipe that scowl off your face. Don't make up your mind about her explanation until you have heard it."

Matt followed her into the café section of the saloon and sat down with her. The table was prepared for the meal and Molly noticed that somehow, Boots had managed to find a small handful of flowers. Well, truth be told they were more weeds than flowers, but they were pretty and they did dress up the table. She again realized how special Boots was and was pondering the fact that she had never really noticed it before when the swinging doors were pushed open and there, in all her quiet humility stood Sierra.

She looked tired and thinner maybe even a little older. But there was a shine in her eyes as she looked at Matt. She didn't move for a moment. She just stood there and took in the picture of her two precious friends sitting at the table. Suddenly her eyes were glistening with the tears that she had swore to herself that she would not shed. She took a deep breath and walked towards them. Both Matt and Molly stood up in unison, as if they were joined together. Molly left the table first and met Sierra half way across the floor. She swept her into her arms and held her tightly. She could feel the upheaval in Sierra's breast as she held her. Molly's eyes welled up and the two friends just stood there holding each other. When they pulled apart, Sierra looked across the room and saw that Matt was still standing by the table. It caught her breath to realize that he had not hurried to say hello.

"Matt. It is so good to see you again. I hope that my note didn't wake you up too early this morning, or yours too Molly. I just felt that this would be the best place to talk."

Matt just stood looking at her. Her voice was the same. She seemed very frail. She had tried to be considerate about the meeting. Why hadn't she been considerate about leaving without a word? He watched her walk toward him and she extended her hand. He took it gently into his realizing that he was holding his breath. He loosened his grip and reached for the back of the chair next to him. He pulled it out and she seated herself in between Matt and Molly. The tension in the air was almost visible. Just like an electrical charge during a thunderstorm.

Boots walked to the table with a pot of fresh brewed coffee and quietly offered his pleasure at seeing her again. He left immediately and for one quiet moment the three friends sat there. Where to begin? Who should begin?

156

"I want to explain to you the reason for my leaving. I can only hope you will understand and forgive me. It all started the night of the dance…"

Chapter 22

... we had such a grand time that night didn't we? I remember how proud I was to be escorted by such a handsome man. I felt the eyes of all the eligible women in town burning into my flesh. Too bad I thought. You had your chance. With all the haughty pride I could muster up, I raised my head high. For the first time in my whole life I was an unutterable snob, and it felt so good. I remember how we danced that slow dance. I couldn't bear to let you have an excuse to dance with anyone else. Fast dancing has never been my thing so I was glad when you told me that you only danced to the slow tunes. Thank you for such a lovely time Matt. I'm sorry. I'm getting away from my story...

... one of the town's building committee members came over and asked you if you had a couple of minutes to spare. He needed to speak to you about a very pressing problem. You left with him and I turned toward the dance floor and watched all the dancers. How colorful all the ladies dresses were. The men looked so handsome in their best suits. My mind was racing. I was thinking about the evening and anxiously awaiting your return. Suddenly, a man put his hand on my arm and called me by name. At first I didn't recognize him, but then with a burst of panic I knew who he was.

You see, many years ago, while just a very young girl I had been married and I had a child. A beautiful little girl! This man had been very abusive both physically and sexually and so I had taken my daughter and run away. I was able to find a wonderful friend who helped me with Annie. She also gave me a job to help pay my way. After I had spent a number of years with her, she decided to retire and she convinced me that I was capable of being able to operate my own business. She needed the cash from the sale of her business in order to live out her retirement. It was such a thriving business and I couldn't afford to buy it from her. I decided to come to Wild River Junction and try my hand at the retail market. Another friend has been taking care of Annie since I left there. I had planned to give myself one year and if I made a go of the business then I would go and bring her here.

Well, suddenly, there was Carl, my husband. He told me that he had known for some time where I had been living. It seems he had a cousin that kept track of Annie. He told me that he was here to take me back to Virginia with him. We were going to get Annie and be a family again. I argued with him. I told him that I didn't believe him about his cousin. He said that if I didn't go with him, he would wire his cousin and Annie would be picked up and brought to Carl's home. Home! He never had a home in his life. He lived in the back rooms of saloons all across the country. He never did a descent or honest days work in his life. I was so scared. I couldn't bear to think of Annie in his hands. I finally told him I would go but only if he promised to leave Annie where she was. He said that he was running from the law and wouldn't want the Wild River Junction sheriff to catch him. He had wired his cousin with the instructions that if he was captured that Annie was to be taken and sold in Mexico City. I made arrangements to meet him at your old homestead Matt. We met early on Sunday morning. All I wanted to do was leave with him so that he would tell his cousin to leave Annie alone. I also believed that I could talk him out of his plan.

I didn't take time to pack anything. I couldn't tell you what I was doing for fear that you would have arrested him Matt, and then Annie would have been in trouble. I ran like a scared rabbit. We spent a couple of days in the farm house. There was no way that I could change his mind. We rode in his old wagon to the water station and got on the train. He left the horses and wagon behind. At Overton we jumped onto an old freight train that was heading to Sweet Tree. We spent the better part of 3 days on that freight car. When we reached the town of Sweet Tree we got off and stayed at the hotel "The Fancy Penny". Nothing fancy about it. There were just enough cowboys and wranglers coming into town all the time that it kept Carl busy playing cards and other money making ventures. He kept me locked up in the room while he was gone. I was beside myself worrying about Annie and then about you two. Knowing you must have felt that I had let you down. I am so sorry.

Anyway! A couple of weeks ago he took me with him to one of the outlying ranches. He made me sit in the wagon while he met with the owner. I don't know what kind of business they had together. Nothing honest I feel. I was in the wagon for quite a long time. There was no one else around that ranch or I would have asked for help. After he came back to the wagon we headed back into town. He seemed a little more anxious than usual. I didn't ask why. I never asked him why about anything. As we were crossing over the river going towards Sweet Tree there was the sound of a shot, and Carl fell over the side of the wagon and lay sprawled in the shallow stream. Blood was running from his mouth and I could see a hole in his chest. Terror totally consumed me. I just knew that I would be the next one to be shot. But I was wrong. Nothing but total silence filled the scenery. I gathered up the reins and urged the horses forward. I could only think that I had to get away from here. If Carl was dead, I was free at last. If he hadn't died from that gun shot, he would certainly die from the exposure of the land. I could just leave him there and no one would be any the wiser. I couldn't breathe. I was in such a state of unsettled feelings. I must have driven the horses a couple of miles before my conscience took over. Slowly I turned the team around and went back to where he was still laying. I jumped down from the wagon and walked over to his soaked body. I placed my hand over his heart and I could feel nothing. I knew then what I had to do. It took all the strength I had, but I was finally able to lift him up onto the bed of the wagon. Then I drove into Sweet Tree and to the sheriff's office. I told him what had happened and he took me over to the undertaker's office. They both removed the body. Not much to say after that. I went back up to our room. I didn't have any money to buy my passage back to Wild River Junction. I didn't even have enough money to pay for the room. The horses and wagon we were using were loaned from someone that Carl had done business with.

I was trying to explain this to the hotel owner, and also hoping he would allow me one more night. All of a sudden the sheriff came up to me and handed me Carl's wallet. I thanked him and walked over to a chair beside the registry table. As I looked into the wallet I saw a thick layer of paper. Looking closer, I discovered that there was a large amount of money in it. Trying to hold back a catch in my voice I told the owner that I was sure I could take care of the bill now. The sheriff told me that he had removed enough money from the wallet to pay for Carl's funeral. He also said that he needed to talk to me regarding exactly what had happened. I promised him that I would be in his office the next morning.

I couldn't shed any light on the shooting. I knew absolutely nothing. I told the sheriff that my husband never told me about his business. I guess I was convincing because he said that there were no charges against me and if I could just remain in Sweet Tree for a couple more days he would appreciate it. After that I could leave anytime I wanted to. And that is exactly what I did. I knew there was another week before the stage would come through, and I couldn't wait. So I bought myself a horse some supplies and with the Sheriff's blessing I rode out of town. It took me five days to get here. But here I am. Again I'm saying that I am so sorry about everything. I only hope that you will forgive me. I don't know what I will do if you don't! It was just the thought of you two that kept me holding together. Without that thought I think I would have gone mad. So. What do you say? Am I forgiven...?

Chapter 23

The silence that followed was as deafening as a clap of thunder. She had told her story. She could only hope that they would believe her. Was it convincing? Did it all fit together? She hoped that she had convinced them.

"Wow! I guess that I can understand why you left in such a hurry. But you have to realize how worried we've been. We even went looking for you." Molly could still remember the terrible days and nights on the trail just praying for any news.

"You went looking for me? Where did you look?"

"Any place we thought you might have gone. Sierra! If you had only left us a note or some kind of a clue before you left. We were frantic with worry. I know it was bad for you, but it was hard on us too."

Matt stood silently watching the two women. The words he was hearing sounded like a drum in his head. One was telling a story that was believable the other finding relief in showing the anxiety she had felt for months now. What about him? What was his reaction? He didn't know for sure.

"Matt?" Sierra turned to face him head on asking the question he was wrangling with. "Do you understand the terrible stress that I was under? I had to do anything and everything to save my daughter. Annie is my total world. She and I have been to hell and back in her short life and I wanted to make sure that she was protected. I didn't know any other way to handle it. It was a total nightmare. The man was a monster. But now he is dead and Annie and I are safe. Please Matt! Say something."

"What do you want me to say Sierra? I've spent the past months in a nightmare of my own. Not knowing what had happened to you was torture. I rode out to the house one day in case you were there. I even found evidence that someone had been there for what looked like several days. Evidently it was you Sierra."

"Matt I already told you that we were there for a while. He wanted some time to work out his plan. He watched me every minute. I couldn't have escaped even if I had wanted to. Matt, you don't know what a cruel vindictive person he was."

"How old were you when you married him?"

"I had just had my thirteenth birthday. I had been living with him and his family for about eight years. I didn't know where my family was. I remember him telling once that my folks didn't want me and that they had sold me to him. His kin were a horrible group. It was my job to take care of them all. I was expected to do everything from the wash to milking the cows. His brothers even thought that I should please them sexually but Carl was saving me for himself. He wanted me to reach the age he thought would bring him the most pleasure. Carl convinced me one day that if I was to marry him he would take me away from it all. There would be just the two of us in our own place. I knew how cruel he was, but it was the lesser of the two evils. Finally I gave in and we ran away and got married. We lived in a dirty little run down hovel just on the outskirts of town in Virginia. Carl drank and gambled all the time. At least he was leaving me alone when he was in town. We were married just a couple of months when the old town midwife told me I was pregnant. I delivered Annie by myself. I was all alone in that shack. Carl was in town at that time. I was fourteen years old. I had begun to forget about my life as it had been before I met him. Each day was a challenge. I was always surprised at the end of each day that I was still alive. Then he began to look at Annie in a way that I remembered him looking at me. I tried to tell myself that it was all my imagination, but then one day I came in the house and found him lying on the bed with her in his arms. She was only three years old. I was petrified. He said he was only hugging her, but I knew better. It was at that time that I decided to get away from him. It's a long story, but I managed to get to Vermont. I met a wonderful women there who helped me and she is the reason that I was able to come here to start a new life. I figured that I would send for Annie when I was sure that my life here could offer her something better than she has now. Matt, please understand why I had to go with him. If he had arranged for his brother to pick her up and bring her to him, the nightmare would only have begun again. I had to do what I needed to do."

"I guess I can understand that Sierra. It's just that…! You see, dammit, I'm in love with you and I couldn't stand the idea that you were in trouble and that I couldn't help you. But now that he's dead, you don't have to live in fear anymore and you can start living again. I'll see to it that you will never be hurt again."

With that said Matt walked over to Sierra and gently took her into his arms. The cruel world was shut out now. The comfort of his arms warmed Sierra to her very soul. The tears in her eyes made everything glisten like diamonds. Matt and Sierra stood locked together in their own world. They didn't hear the light steps of Molly as she quietly walked out of the room. She closed the door and sighed. At least something good had come from this terrible event. Knowing that she wouldn't be seeing either Sierra or Matt for a while, she walked into her saloon. Boots was standing just inside the door and she walked over to him and gently leaned against him. Instinctively he put his arms around her and held her. He didn't know what had happened to bring her to him this way, and he didn't care. One never questions a small piece of heaven.

Chapter 24

"God's in his heaven and all's right with the world". For the first time in many years Sierra realized that this applied to her. Matt loved her and she returned that love two fold. He finally knew the truth – well, almost all the truth. There are some things that she must keep inside, buried somewhere deep down in the darkness. She felt a small gnawing of a conscience that she had long ago thought to be dead. "Go away!" she cried, "I don't need you to spoil things for me now. Things are going to be perfect from now on. Go back to that place where you've been hiding."

As the sun had risen that morning Sierra had left the bed that she had shared with Matt for the first time. What a wondrous night it had been. There had been a gentle unveiling of their eager bodies. The feel of Matt's hands on her skin. Soft! Yes, definitely soft, and yet rough enough to make the night exciting. Never had she been treated with so much love and tenderness. Now she could understand what that special thing between a man and a woman really was. Nothing to be afraid of, nothing causing pain, only that exciting wave of emotion that had erupted from her body. That feeling that had lay dormant for all these years. She finally felt like a real woman. She looked down as Matt lay there sleeping. Her heart cried out from inside of her. Her happiness totally engulfed her. "Sleep my love," she said silently, "when you awake we will make this new life a special beginning."

By the time she had the coffee perked and the ham and eggs were in the pan, cooking. Matt began stretching out from under the covers. He hadn't slept this late in years, but he didn't want to get out of bed and break the spell that seemed to have hold of him. Her perfume lay gently on the pillows and he inhaled deeply, taking her in. "I just have to get up," he said to himself. "We have so many plans to make now. I'll never let her out of my sight again. We are going to be together forever."

He put his arms around her waist as she stood at the stove and laid his head on her back.

"There will never be another night that you and I are apart." Matt promised.

"That makes sense to me," replied Sierra. "But Matt, before we make plans for ourselves we must remember Annie. I want to get her here as soon as possible. I don't want to take a chance that Carl did have a cousin watching her. You don't know that family. They're all crazy and vindictive. If his cousin finds out that Carl is dead I know he will try to get to Annie. I have to go back to Vermont and bring her here. I can't expect her to travel all that distance alone."

"Of course you can't. After breakfast we'll check the schedule at the train station and make plans accordingly. You might want to wire your friend too and tell her to have everything ready for you. That way you won't have to spend any more time away from me than is absolutely necessary."

The morning flew by for the two lovers. They resented the fact that there was a real world outside, one that they would have to join soon. They managed to steal a few more hours before Matt had to leave for his office.

* * * *

The following days were a whirlwind of activity for both of them. There was so much to arrange for Sierra's trip. A wire had been sent to Arletta telling her that Sierra would be coming for Annie in just a couple of weeks. A return wire from Arletta had set Sierra's mind at ease. She had stated that Annie was doing fine and that she would keep close watch on her until Sierra arrived. Matt had decided that when Annie came to them that they should be living in the farm house.

"A little girl needs a room of her own with pretty curtains on the windows and lots of dolls lying around. Maybe even a puppy romping in the yard."

Sierra had loved him even more when she heard him say this. They decided that Sierra would postpone the trip for two weeks. That way the house would be almost finished and Matt could take care of anything else that he felt needed to be done while she was away. They had discussed the merits of getting married before Sierra left or waiting for when she returned. If they waited then Annie could be part of the celebration. On the other hand, if they were not married when she got here, then Matt would have to live at the jail house until such a time as they could be together legally.

This last idea didn't go over so well with Matt, but he would have done it if it was what Sierra wanted. She thought endlessly about this decision. Maybe it would be better to bring Annie into an already stable environment. Sierra had no doubt that Annie would love Matt. And he was so excited to have this child as part of his life too.

"What do you think Sierra?" Was a question that Matt asked.

"What do I think about what, Matt?'

"Do you think she will call me Dad, Father or even Pop?"

"Gosh Matt! I don't know. What would you like her to call you?'

"I'm afraid she'll call me Matt."

"Well, that is your name. But I doubt she'll do that. Guess we'll have to wait and see."

The big decision was finally made. Matt and Sierra would be married in two weeks, the day before she left to pick up Annie. This pleased Matt very much.

Molly of course was to be a part of the celebration. She had offered to have the wedding reception in the saloon and she would pay for it as her wedding present. Both Molly and Sierra spent time deciding on the decorations and designing Sierra's wedding dress. An ivory satin was chosen and a simple dress was the design. Nothing fancy, Sierra had stated. A bolt of lace material that Sierra found in the general store was used to make the veil and the headdress was made from pearl beads that Isabel Stoneman had found tucked away under the counter in her store.

A round trip train ticket was purchased for Sierra and a one way ticket for Annie. All the plans were coming together. The whole town seemed to get involved with the planning and everyone was so excited.

Old Rose MacAffee, from the boarding house took charge of inviting everyone. Those that she couldn't walk to in town she just put on her best calico dress and borrowed a wagon from Gabe Rogers and rode all over the area. This was one lady that never ceased to amaze Sierra. There seemed to be no job too difficult for her to handle. Old Martha and Violet offered to help with the cooking for the reception and also to make the wedding cake. The reverend Potter was the one that had the license to marry them. Gabe Rogers volunteered to dress up an old carriage for the bride to ride in to the church. The pastor had entered the date into his church journal which now made it official. It sounded just like your normal everyday wedding, but to Sierra, it was heaven on earth and nothing was going to intrude on her special day.

Matt's work on the house was going right on time. He had hired Pat Grady to help him and the kid worked like a fiend. Everything was repaired, painted and even a new roof crowned the beauty of the home. A new porch would be built while Sierra was away getting Annie. Matt had already planned to put a double porch swing on it. This would be enjoyed during the evenings while they watched the sun go down over the hills. It seemed that everything was running ahead of schedule. Matt couldn't wait until he and Sierra and little Annie lived in this house that had belonged to his folks. "It's gonna make pop and mom real happy. I know they're still a part of this house. They were so happy here. I can almost feel them whenever I come into the kitchen. I have even imagined that I could smell mom's apple pie. They would be so happy to see how this has all come together. The farm looks almost as it had when mom and Pop lived here. I think they are proud of me. I only hope so."

As Matt turned around to close the front door he was sure that he caught a glimpse of a shadow among the trees. He smiled to himself. "Yep! I knew you were here Pop!"

Chapter 25

"You were married once, Boots. What was it like?" Matt questioned.

"Gosh! It's been a lot of years past since then. I do remember that I was only happy when I was doing something to please Charity. She was so easy to live with. She had a sweet innocence about her. She was 15 when I met her and only 16 when we married. I had to do some fast talking to her father in order for it to happen. I remember I talked to him at a church picnic. I was so nervous. I had made up my mind that if he said no, then we were going to run away together. I guess that he understood how much I loved her. His only objection was that my future looked a little bleak as I didn't have any land or any kind of a home to take her to. I remember promising him that within one year I would have a working farm with a house on it. I really wasn't sure how I was going to do it, but it was important enough to me that I keep my word. We had waited for one year and during that time I was able to find steady work. I saved my earnings then one day I found out that one of the town's people had decided to give up farming. I went out to see him and we made a deal and I bought his spread. It wasn't a thriving farm but I knew that with time it could be. But it was mine and so, soon, was Charity. We were both so proud of it. She worked side by side with me for a couple of years. You couldn't imagine a tiny thing like that being able to help dig a new well or repair a fence. She even helped put the roof on. It wasn't until she was expecting Zack that I could talk her into taking it easy. We used to laugh a lot. We also made love a lot too. There is such closeness when two people create a lifestyle and watch it grow. When our son, Zack was born our life became richer and fuller. He was so special to us. We didn't believe that we could have any more children and then eight years later, along came John. What a thrill! We thought our family was complete. But then, well, fate took over and suddenly it was all gone. But did I like being married? Yes! I would do it again if a certain someone would acknowledge my existence. Yes, I sure would, in a heart beat."

"Well, I guess that helps me a lot. I never dreamed that I would be so nervous. I've never committed to anyone before. But this feels so right. I have such strong feelings for Sierra. I know that we can make it work. She's had a tough life and I feel that she is entitled to all the wonders that life can bring. I'm anxious to meet her daughter. If she is anything like Sierra, she will be a treasure. O.K. Boots! Let's get this over with. Walk me to my favorite girl and be there to hold me down if I decide to run. Thanks Boots, for talking to me. I know how difficult it is for you to think back on your life."

* * * *

Thinking back difficult? Yes. But the future seemed to be a brighter place right now for Boots. He smiled as he remembered the incident this morning. He had been standing behind the bar, getting ready for this afternoons celebration when Molly came down the stairs. Sweet Molly! There was no doubt in his mind the effect that she had on him. She only had to walk close by and he would feel like a young man looking for his beloved, and finding her, melted onto the floor. In Molly's hand was a letter. She had made a real production about giving it to him.

"Boots, this was included with the mail when I picked everything up today. I didn't notice that this was yours until I had slit it open. I assure you that I did not read it. I wanted to; I admit that my curiosity almost got the better of me. After all, you've never received any kind of mail since I've known you. Well, just take this and read it. I'll be over there eating my breakfast if you have anything you want to talk about."

The letter in his hand gave Boots a feeling of apprehension. The only person that would write to him was his son Zack. Unless someone who knew Zack was sending bad news to him. He looked for several moments at the envelope. What had once been white was now a brownish color due to the dust from the travels of this document. In the upper right hand corner was an address that Boots didn't recognize. Sweet Tree, Nebraska! The handwriting was very feminine but with a bold flair to it. He hesitated again to open it. Rolling it around in his hands he caught a slight perfume in the air. It was very slight. Almost like something that Charity would have worn.

"You know Boots you'll wear that envelope out with your turning and twisting it around. So open it for heaven's sake. I also caught the hint of perfume on it. Is there somebody you haven't told me about?"

Molly asked the question with a slight hesitation. Not knowing the answer to her question she realized that she was nervous as to the answer. She found that her heart was beating a little faster than normal.

"O.K. Molly, you caught me. I have a secret love life that I keep hidden from you. I do it all in my spare time away from this place. Here, I'll show you that I have no one that I haven't told you about. Move over and let me sit at your table and I'll read you the letter."

"You don't have to do that Boots. I was only joking. You have a right to your privacy. But, if you insist, I'm ready."

As Boots pulled the chair away from the table he turned it and placed it with the back to Molly. He straddled the seat and leaning on the back he tore open the envelope and pulled out several pages. With a raspy voice, he cleared the phlegm from his throat and began:

Sunday, April 25

Dear Mr. Webber;

I know that you are going to be surprised when you receive this letter. I am writing this for myself and for my husband Zack. Your son Zack! He is not one to put pen to paper and so I decided that I would help him in this instance.

First of all let me assure you that Zack is well and in good health. We have been married for three years now and have recently become the proud parents of a beautiful girl. We named her Marie. Yes! You have a granddaughter.

Zack's job has caused him to travel frequently and as of 2 months ago we have been living in this lovely town of Sweet Tree. However, we are once again having to pack up and move.

As our new destination is bringing us close to where you live we will be stopping by so that you and Zack can become acquainted again and also so that you can meet your new granddaughter. I have such high hopes that you and I will be friends.

We will be arriving in six days. I sincerely hope that this is good news for you.

Your loving family,

Zack, Pamela and Marie Webber

"Oh! My gosh Boots! You have a granddaughter. How excited you must feel right now!

What was the date on the letter? We have to get ready for them. Where will they stay?"

Molly sounded as confused as Boots felt right now. A granddaughter! That's another generation of Webbers. And imagine his Zack wanting to come here and see him. Boot's thoughts were running all over the place.

"Let me see, the letter is dated Sunday April 25. That means they will be here on May 1st. OH! No! That's today! How am I going to get things ready for them in time? And today is the wedding too. I'm supposed to go over and give Matt some last minute courage in a couple of hours. Molly! How am I going to do it?"

"Just simmer down grandpa. There is only one place they can stay and that's at MacAffee's Boarding house. I have to go and help Sierra get ready for the wedding in a couple of hours and so before I go there I'll go to Mrs. MacAffee's and get things set up. She's helping with the wedding, but the way she keeps the rooms in her house she won't have to do anything but open the windows."

"Wow! Thanks Molly. I don't know what I would do without you. You are a special and treasured friend. Now I'd better go and find my best suit and lay it out. I wonder who will be the most nervous, me or Matt?"

"That's a good question, grandpa. Wow! A grand-daughter! And you get a new daughter too. She sure sounds like a terrific person Boots. This will be a day that we will always remember. Before you go, let's have a toast to the new family. No. I don't mean with booze. I mean with coffee. Here's to your new family, Boots." Molly raised her cup and eyed Boots over the edge of the rim. "He looks scarred to death," she thought. "It's been a lot of years since he's seen his son. But then, Boots is a very different man now. He's a sweet, wonderful man who deserves all the happiness that he can get. Maybe someday I'll be able to add to his happiness. Gee, listen to me. I've just realized that he's very important to me. I think I love him. No! I don't think. I know I do. Wow! When did that happen? Two seconds ago I was just this ordinary person and now here I am acknowledging the fact that I'm in love. I'm beginning to know how Sierra feels. Well, when this wedding is over maybe Boots and I can talk about a future together. I really hope for that."

With loving thoughts running through her head Molly headed up the stairs to her rooms and stared at the outfit hanging on the door. This was the dress that she was to wear to Sierra's wedding. Maybe the next time she prepared for a big occasion it would be her wedding dress of white satin covered with silken roses, hanging on the door. In her mind's eye, Molly could see the apparition. She could almost reach out and touch it.

* * * *

"Well, Molly. What do you think? Will Matt be happy with the way his bride looks?"

"If he isn't, he isn't the man I've known for all these years. You look beautiful Sierra. I don't know how you made that gown in such a short time, but it's perfect. I doubt that Wild River has ever seen such a beautiful bride. I'm gonna feel like an old hag standing next to you."

"Oh Molly! There is nothing old or hag looking about you. You are a gorgeous woman. Everyone in town thinks that. Especially one very devoted employee. You know if you would give Boots half a chance you could have this same happiness that I feel right now. I bet he would make a great husband. He sure loves you enough."

"What? He does not! We're just good friends. At least that's the way I think of him."

"Yeah, sure you do. Come on Molly you aren't kidding anyone. I guess I'll have to work on getting you two together after I come home with Annie."

"You just leave the two of us alone. We're doing just fine thank you."

"By the way Molly, where is Boots? I thought he would be here to ride with you to the church."

"Oh, I guess that I didn't tell you. He got a letter from his son this morning. It said that they're going to be here sometime today. Boots is trying to hide the fact that he's excited, but you can tell he is. My guess is that he's a little nervous to. While he's waiting he went down to Matt's. He wanted to be sure that the groom didn't pack a bag and run."

"Good for Boots. It would be embarrassing if there was a bride and no groom. And what do you mean 'they' will be here?"

"The letter was from his daughter-in-law. It seems that she and Zack have been married for three years and they have a lovely new baby girl. Boots is so excited. I've never seen him so happy. I hope it works out for him and his son. It's been a lot of years since they've seen each other."

"Maybe mine and Matt's luck has been passed on. I sure hope that things work out for them. Well, Molly my love, by the sounds of the horse and carriage out front, I do believe that it is time for us to go. Give me a hug Molly. I really need to have someone's arms around me right now to hold me down on the ground. I fear I might just float out of here and into the church. You've been a very special friend to me Molly and I have to tell you that I love you most dearly."

"That goes both ways my dear friend. I've never had a female friend that I felt so close to. It was always something that I laughed about when I used to see other women being so close. But now I realize how grand it is to have someone to talk to and laugh with. Someone that understands me! I hope we will always have that special feeling that only comes from true friendship."

The two grown women extended the intimate moment just a little longer and then in silence they walked to the door of the dress shop and gasped at the sight that met them there. Old Gabe Rogers had painted the wagon with white wash and then, threaded through the spokes of the wheels, were ribbons of all colors. Across the top of the wagon were bunches of wildflowers tied on. The old man himself was dressed in his best suit and as Sierra approached him, he held out his hand to help her onto the wagon. She quickly pulled him to her and threw her arms around his neck. She kissed him on the cheek then whispered into his ear that he was the most wonderful and handsomest of men. He then gently lifted her onto the wagon seat. Then he extended his hand to Molly and as she hoisted herself into the wagon she could feel the warmth of old Gabe's grin. He cautiously climbed onto the driver's seat and gently touched the backs of the horses with his crop. He wanted no problems today. He had very special cargo to carry to a very special event.

Chapter 26

A small wagon entered Wild River Junction at a slow pace. Looking at the horse you could tell that they had traveled many miles. The man and woman sitting on the wagon glanced around them. They noticed that there didn't seem to be many people around. The street had a ghostly atmosphere. Most of the shops had closed signs on them. How curious! What incident had led all these people to leave their places of business locked up so early in the day?

"Maybe someone important died." The handsome young lady said. "You know, Zack, sometimes people do that."

"What? People die?"

"No silly. If somebody important dies and they have a big funeral then everyone in town goes to pay their last respects."

"Well, I doubt if the owners of the saloon has closed up. They never do. That's where we're supposed to go. It seems strange to me that a man who is an alcoholic would work around a saloon. Unless he's drinking every other drink he pours then it would be heaven to him. Remember, I told you that my father almost died from alcohol. He lived with this demon for years. I really don't see how he could have straightened himself out. Oh well. I guess we'll see. I think I remember that we turn left at the end of the street."

The old horse plodded its way down the street and then went in a northerly direction. Anyone seeing the old hag would wonder how it could pull the wagon. But Zack knew that the animal had a big heart and would not fail them. If the time ever came that he could buy a piece of property he would put the poor old thing out to pasture. It had given him many years of loyalty. He had won it in a card game and the poor thing was old at that time. No one seemed to know how old, but all you had to do was look it over and you knew it was close to the end. But Zack had been kind to her and so had been able to coax a couple more years of service from her.

They pulled to a stop in front if the Wild River Saloon. Still nothing stirred. There was only a slight breeze that came across from the river. Suddenly the faint strains of an organ fell into their ears.

"Oh, Zack listen! There must be a church close by. I can hear organ music. That must be the reason that no one is around."

"Yeah, I hear it. Let me look in the saloon and see if anyone is here."

Zack jumped down from the wagon and walked up the steps to the saloon door. A note had been pinned to it. It stated that the saloon was closed for an hour and asked anyone who wanted inside to come back later.

"Well, no one is here. I guess we could just sit here and wait."

"Zack, I have a better idea. It's a little chilly out here and I don't want the baby exposed to the wind. She might catch a cold and we don't want that. Why don't we go over to the church and go inside. At least there will be a little warmth."

"What a smart gal I married. Sure we can do that Pamela. It beats sitting out here."

Picking up the reins Zack encouraged the old horse to once more start walking. They followed the strains of the music and quickly found the church. It set up on a little knoll and shone white in the light of day. The steeple was crowned with a giant cross and just underneath the steeple was a bell tower. Pam could only imagine how wonderful the ringing of the bell would sound. She was instantly attracted to this little town. How bad could a town be if it had such a beautiful church with a bell! She imagined herself and Zack walking through the doors on a Sunday morning holding the hand of young Marie. She would be greeting all of their friends and they would be invited to Sunday dinner. Pam let herself indulge in this fantasy. It was something she really wanted. Since she had married Zack they had moved from one place to another. They had never stayed long enough for her to become a part of the townspeople. Zack had promised her right after Marie was born that he would look for a place to settle down. This visit to his father was part of this promise. Zack was going to see if his father knew of any farm that could be bought cheaply. After all, Boots had been living in this area for several years now and would probably know. That is, if Boots was sober. She hoped that he would be.

The music from the organ had stopped. They opened the door without making a sound and quickly found a seat in the back row.

"And do you Sierra take this man to be your husband?"

"I do."

"I now pronounce you husband and wife. Matt you may kiss your bride."

The white veil was lifted and Sierra's shining face was lifted up to meet that of her husband's. A quick kiss and the couple turned towards their friends. Smiles and tears showed from all that had gathered in the church.

They walked down the aisle towards the door and with beaming faces looked around the seated congregation, not wanting to miss anyone. They smiled at all, even the strangers in the back row. How radiant Sierra looked and her eyes spoke of the happiness she felt in her heart.

"Oh my goodness Zack, look who it is! It's See See!" This exclamation from Pamela echoed across the aisle. "Can you imagine that our paths have crossed again?"

"It's hard to believe. I never thought that we would see her again. And look Pamela, Boots is here. That's why no one was at the saloon."

At the door the bridal couple waited for their guests to emerge from the church and then met them with love and appreciation. Each one of these people expressed their congratulations and wished the couple well. It was such a happy moment for Matt and Sierra. How can two people be so very lucky and have such wonderful friends and neighbors. This would be a day that the couple would remember forever.

As the last of the people came through the doors, Sierra noticed that Boots was hugging the stranger that had been sitting in the back row. Strange, she thought. It must be someone that Boots knows. Then Boots picked up a little bundle from the pew and looked at it with loving eyes. Wrapped up in a beautiful pink blanket was a baby. Boots held the small bundle as if it would break. He was so gentle. And as this moment was passing the woman turned around and smiled at Sierra.

"I thought that we would never see you again See See. We never imagined that when we chose to come here to see Boots that we would see you too. Congratulations on your marriage. We wish you a long and happy life. Heaven knows you deserve it after all that happened. We must get together soon."

* * * *

It was hard to breathe. She couldn't seem to get the air into her lungs. Panic set in and she wanted to run. She knew she couldn't. Probably her legs wouldn't let her move anyway. Why had this happened? This was supposed to be her day. Everything was supposed to go beautifully. Nothing was supposed to happen to mar her happiness. Matt looked down at her and saw that her face was white as a sheet. Too much excitement he thought. She was probably exhausted. He turned towards her and lifted her up into his arms and put her up onto the bridal wagon. He ran around the other side and stepped up, grabbing the reins as he went. He headed the horses towards the saloon and stole a quick look at his new bride's face.

"Sierra? Are you alright? You're so pale. Are you sick, excited or hungry? What is it dear? You're scaring me."

"I guess I must be a little excited and hungry. I'm sorry I scared you. It was just that…"

"And who was that lady that seemed to know you? She called you See See. Do you know her?"

"I don't remember her. She must be mistaken. There must be someone out there that looks like me. I feel sorry for her, that poor dear."

"Nonsense, she's a very lucky and beautiful woman. Do you feel that you can go to the saloon for the party?"

"Of course I can. I wouldn't dream of standing up all our friends. Matt, the church was packed. Everyone in town was there. Wasn't that a beautiful wedding? How wonderful that so many people came to help us celebrate this special day."

"I noticed that Boots knew the people in the back row. I bet it was Boot's son and wife. They were to be in town today. They have a small baby with them. How exciting for him. Just found out today that he's a grandfather."

"Matt, can we just stay a short while at the saloon. I think maybe I should go back to the shop and rest. I don't want to get over tired for my trip tomorrow. Annie wouldn't like her mom to be ill when she came for her. You can go back to the saloon and enjoy the party, but I just want to rest. Would that be alright?"

"Of course it would be alright. But I don't want to go back to the party without you. I'll stay with you in case you need something."

"No Matt. Please! Promise me you will go back. I won't rest if I know you're missing out on our celebration. Besides, all our friends will expect us to be there. You can represent both of us. Please!"

"Well I'll think about it. Just one quick visit with everyone and then you're going to go home. That's doctor's orders and a new husband's request."

"I thank you doctor. Matt, please promise me something. Always remember that I love you very much. No matter what happens, don't believe anything else but that I love you with all my heart."

"There is nothing going to happen that will make me doubt your love for me, just as I hope that you will never doubt my love for you."

"Thank you Matt."

The door to the saloon was open and several people were waiting for the bride and groom. As the couple passed them they were pelted with a shower of rice and shouts of congratulations. One gruff voice started singing "Here comes the bride, all fat and wide. Here comes the bridegroom as thin as a pin." These resonant tones were met with hearty laughter.

Chapter 27

The door to the boarding house banged shut as Boots kicked at it.

"Mrs. MacAfee said it was the third door on the right, just one flight up. That woman sure keeps her house in tip top shape."

The furniture sparkled from the shine that was a constant feature in the MacAffee house. Years of elbow grease had brought the grain of the wood to the surface and the delicate pattern's lay there just below the shine. Most of the furniture had been brought here by Mrs. MacAffee's parents. She had remembered as a child the stories of their crossing the country in a covered wagon that was loaded down with these same treasures. They had been her mother's dowry and nothing was going to stop her from bringing everything she had with her. Her mother had told her that when her father had asked her to marry him and go west with him her answer had been held up until she knew for sure that she could take these treasures with her. It was only then that she had said yes.

Boot's family walked into the spacious room. They were astounded at the light that flooded the area. Two very large windows at the front overlooked the busy street below and an enormous bed in between them. The feather comforter that covered the bed looked as if you could get lost in the depth of it. Boots was so grateful to Mrs. MacAffee for her choice of this room. His beautiful new 'daughter' and granddaughter looked at home in these surroundings.

Zack set the suitcase on a little stand and looked around. He could not have picked anything better if he had picked it himself.

"Well Pam, do you think you will be comfortable here for a couple of days?"

It was the smile on her face that gave him the answer before he saw it in her eyes.

"It's just perfect Zack. This is such a lovely room. We can get a wooden crate from the country store that I saw as we came by and make it into a crib for Marie. We can set it on top of that chest of drawers. That should suit her just fine. Thank you Boots for arranging all of this."

She walked over to Boots and gave him a quick hug and a peck on the cheek. What an outgoing personality she has, Boots was thinking. I think I'll enjoy having her in this family.

"There is one thing I am confused about though," Pamela stated. "It's about See See. Why are they calling her Sierra? And why is she getting married already when she just buried her husband? I'm so confused. Can you explain any of this Boots?"

"Actually, Pamela, I can't. I thought that I knew Sierra pretty well but I just can't explain it. Are you sure that you aren't getting her mixed up with someone that looks just like her? When you spoke to her at the church I got the distinct impression that she didn't know you. Besides, I don't know the story as to how you think you know her."

"Under the circumstances of our meeting", she said to Boots "believe me I would never forget her."

Zack knew that there was about to be revealed a secret that he felt maybe should stay hidden, but then he had come this far to begin a new relationship with his father and he felt that he owed the truth to Boots.

"Enough time for all of this Pamela. Why don't you unpack the suitcase and then take a little rest. You have to be tired after riding in the wagon for so long. And I know that you didn't sleep well last night. I'll just go with Boots and we can get re-acquainted. Maybe we can talk out the hurt of the past number of years. What do you say Boots? Want to walk around town and show me the place?"

"I would be very happy to do that son."

* * * *

Boots and Zack walked at a slow pace and covered one end of town to the other. Small talk was the menu. Nothing serious, just cautious baby steps of intimacy being bared. Then they began to talk of Boots' years of degradation, of his being held fast by the promises of the alcohol, the promises that if he kept at it, it would totally take away the terrible hurt and emptiness that he had felt deep down inside him. The promises that if he kept at it he would be able to forget the image of his wife mutilated and raped lying on the floor of their home, the image of his little baby boy, lying in the dirt, torn to pieces by some animal, the total lack of caring for himself, only the thought of where the next drink was going to come from.

Then there had been the years of not knowing or caring, as to who he was or even where he was. Death would have been kinder. He had welcomed the idea of death as a means to be with his family again. It was at this time that he had been rescued by his guardian angel. She took him in she taught him to care about himself and others. She boxed his ears when he slipped back once or twice, and then rewarded him when he was totally saved from the demon alcohol. Molly had saved his life and he would be forever grateful to her. She had given him a job in the saloon, nothing much at first, but then as he caused her no more anxiety about being around the bar she gave him one more test. Showing her trust in him she had asked him to tend the bar. He had never let her down. He never even thought about the alcohol anymore. Just served it and watched what it did to others. He had even found himself lecturing different people about the dangers of drinking too much. Every once in a while after one of this lectures he would notice Molly standing off in the distance with a smirk on her face.

He cleared the air with all of his confession to Zack. He stated that he knew that he had not been a good father. And for that he would always be sorry. He felt as if he had stolen not only his life with the drinking, but Zack's life as well.

"I know that you have much to be angry with me for Zack, but if you could forgive me and give me another chance. I will do anything that I can to help you and your family. Just tell me what I can do. I want you to know that your coming here today means more to me than anything else in this world. It is so hard for me to realize that you're now a married man with a beautiful wife and daughter."

"Boots, I have to admit that it's taken a lot of persuasion by Pamela for me to come here. I've been knocking around this big country for a number of years. I've done some things that I'm not particularly proud of, but then I may have done a few things right. I wasn't ready to settle down. I just wanted to wander all over and take whatever came my way. Then I met Pamela. I had been playing cards with her father. He owned a small farm just outside of town. His addiction was gambling. He would make a bet at the drop of a hat. On this one particular night he ran out of money and placed the deed to his farm on the table. He was so sure that he couldn't lose. He was wrong. I won the pot. I had all the money and his farm. Afterwards, he said that he really didn't mean to do it and that I couldn't take the farm away from him. There were enough witness's there that finally he had to concede. I picked up my winnings and was

188

on my way. Having that deed in my hand did something to me. It felt so good to finally own something. It surprised me. I had figured I would go on roaming forever. I was so anxious to see the place that a couple of days later I rode out there. The man was no where around. Evidently he had left town after the game and nobody knew where he was. I met his wife and daughter. I asked them where he was and they said that they hadn't seen him for over a week, but that that was nothing unusual. Sometimes he would be gone for months at a time if he was on a winning streak. The farm was rundown and needed a lot of work. I explained to the two of them that I now owned the farm and that I wanted to move into it. The shock on their faces hit me to my very foundation. They had no idea. He had never told them. After a couple of minutes the mother composed herself enough to realize the dire situation that she was in. She asked me into the house and she poured me a cup of coffee. She asked if she and her daughter could have until the end of the month to get another place. Of course I gave my permission. In the next number of days I saw both of them in town frequently. They were desperately seeking information regarding anything that would be available for them to live in. There were only a couple of days left before the deadline and I had gone to the farm again. They had both been loading up a small wagon with their personal possessions. They were hot and tired and eager for this job to be done. I helped with some of the heavier items, and just as we had loaded everything possible that the wagon could hold I stopped dead in my tracks. I whirled around and saw the sadness and frustration on their faces. I inquired as to where they were going and then I suddenly realized that they weren't going any place in particular. Evidently they had not been able to find a place to live. They were just going to get in the wagon and go. Two women, on their own, riding across the plains to heaven knows what. I realized that I couldn't do it. I made them help me take the stuff out of the wagon and put it back in the house. I told the mother that I would keep the deed to the farm, and that I would start working at getting it back into order again. Meanwhile, I would like her and her daughter to live in the house and help take care of things. You cannot believe the tears that flowed from those two women. They had been scared to death about leaving, but would have if it was what they had had to do. I made them promise me that should the husband return, they were to get word to me and I would make sure that he was put off the land. It seemed to please them that he wouldn't be there to bother them anymore. I told them that any money they made regarding chickens, eggs or the chickens themselves, they could keep. Anyway, to make a long story short, I spent a lot of time at the farm. Was out there some to fix it up, but mostly to be in the company of the daughter, Pamela. Yeah! That's right. I knew I had a winner and was not about to let her go. About six months after we were married, her mother died. The farm was a losing proposition. The dirt had no nutrients in the soil and nothing would grow. So we sold the farm and decided that we should look for something else. We've been traveling around for a long time now. I knew we had to settle down when Pamela became pregnant. I was hoping that we would have found something by the time the baby came, but it didn't happen. After she had the baby I promised her that we would come here and see if you could help us find a new place. She needs a stable life. She is a good wife and a wonderful mother. I love her so much. So now you know the whole story. What do you think Boots? Do you know of any place around here that would suit us?"

The glimmer of a thought crossed Boot's mind. In the business that he was in he was always hearing about this one and that one wanting to sell, or not being able to keep up with the payments on their property. He would start paying more attention to the conversations he'd have with his customers.

"Zack, right at this moment I don't know of any place, but I would be very proud to help you. And if I don't hear of anything, I just bet that Molly or Matt will know. Just stay at Mrs. MacAffee's until we find something. Maybe we can find some kind of a job for you until we get you a farm. You're going to need to work to feed those two beautiful women of yours. Now, let's go into the saloon and you can have a beer and I'll have a cup of coffee. I want to hear the story of how you met Sierra."

Chapter 28

It must have been around daybreak when Sierra opened her eyes. For one brief moment she felt anxious. Looking around the room she saw that Matt hadn't come to bed. Everything was so still and quiet. She wondered where he was.

"Must have been quite a party they had. He probably stayed at the saloon so that he wouldn't disturb me. But then, it was our wedding night. Or could it have been that he had talked to that young couple. Oh, dear God…!"

The panic in her heart surged forth like a shot.

"Maybe he decided not to come to me at all. Maybe I've lost him forever. What in the world should I do? I'm supposed to leave in a couple of hours for the east and I don't know where my husband is."

Dressing in an automatic rhythm, not paying any attention to what she was doing, Sierra knew in her heart that her world was about to come tumbling down. As she walked across the room she heard the front door of the shop open. The little bell echoed loudly. It rang louder than it ever had before. It seemed like hours before the bedroom door opened up.

It moved slowly. Then, the sight of Matt caused her knees to buckle and she fell to the floor. He cautiously walked over to her and leaning down he took hold of her hand and gently pulled her to her feet.

"Are you alright Sierra?"

"Yes. I guess that I am more tired than I realized. Yesterday was quite a day."

"Yes. I agree with you. It was a day that I will always remember. Sierra! Why didn't you tell me the truth about your husband's death?"

"I did Matt. I told you he had been killed."

"Yes, we both know that he was killed. You just never told us the truth of it nor how it came about and your part in his life."

"I don't understand Matt. What are you getting at?"

"I spent the night with Boots and his son. That's where I found out what happened. It's nothing like you told Molly and me. Why did you have to lie about it? I love you and I would have tried to understand whatever it was."

"Oh, Matt? How can you believe a stranger against me? I'm your wife. Doesn't that account for anything?"

"Of course it does. But I know you lied to me. I just don't understand why. Don't you trust me?"

"I trust you. But for some reason you don't seem to trust me. Here I am getting ready to leave to fetch my daughter and your accusing me of heaven knows what. Well maybe I will just have to trust that you will come to your senses while I'm gone. Now please, put that suitcase into the wagon and drive me to the station!"

"No Sierra. Your trip will have to wait until we have time to sort this thing out. There is something very wrong here and we need to get it solved."

"Your right, there is something very wrong. I have a new husband and he is already ordering me around, telling me what I can and can't do. Where I can go and where I can't go. Where is the trust we spoke about yesterday? You are being totally idiotic and if you don't wish to believe me then that is your problem. Maybe it will be best if I go back east and stay there. You can get an annulment from the judge and we'll be done with this relationship."

"Oh, no you don't. You don't get out of this that easy."

"What are you going to do, bind my hands and feet and tie me to a chair?"

"That's an idea. I'll do it if I have to. Just make up your mind Sierra that this time I want the truth. No long stories that sound good. I want the truth. Damn! I deserve the truth."

She knew that he was right. He did deserve the truth. No matter how much it may cost her. She hung her head down and looked at the floor. There would be no lying this time. The truth had to be told whether she wanted him to hear it or not. She knew that the truth would bring an end to all the dreams that she had fought so strongly to achieve.

"Alright, Matt, I'll tell you the whole sordid story. God help me when I do."

Matt walked over to her and put his arms gently around her and held her close. He loved her so much and he knew that no matter what she told him he would forgive her and still love her.

"Matt, if I'm going to do this, then I need to be honest with everyone. Walk with me to the saloon and get Molly and Boots to join us. They've been an important part of my life for so long. I want to include them in my story. And this is a story that I will only ever tell just one time."

Holding on to Matt's hand, watching her feet glide across the ground, she felt as if she was in another world. It seemed like forever before they approached the saloon and took each step up into the doorway. Matt pushed the doors apart and led her to a table that still had the remnants of last night's party scattered about on it. He seated her into a chair and stepped aside. He walked over to the staircase and called.

Boots was the first to answer.

"Hey! Matt! Didn't expect to see you so soon today and there's Sierra with you. Sorry about the shape of the place, but I just got up a few minutes ago myself. Molly said that we were going to stay closed until this evening. We all needed our rest before we tackled this mess. How about some coffee? I just brewed a pot. I don't know about you, but I sure need the boost."

"Boots, do you think that Molly is up yet?"

"Oh, yes. I can hear her walking around upstairs. She never sleeps late. Want me to go and get her?"

"I'd sure appreciate it. We want to talk to both Molly and you."

"Wow! Sounds serious! I'll go and get her."

He made his way over to the stairway. The carpet on the stairs muffled his footsteps as he rose up one runner at a time. Reaching the landing he turned left and knocked at the first door.

"Molly? Are you decent? I have to talk to you. I think it's important."

Molly opened the door and with a questioning look faced Boots.

"What's the matter?"

"Well, I don't rightly know, but Matt and Sierra are downstairs and they both look like they just lost their best friends. I spent a lot of time with Matt and Zack last night and I am guessing that this has something to do with what Zack was talking about. I had intended to tell you today, but haven't had a chance yet."

"Tell me what?"

"Well, let's see what they have to say and then I'll tell you later."

"You sure have my curiosity piqued. O.K., give me about five minutes and I'll be down. See if they want any breakfast, or at least coffee."

"That's all taken care of. I'll go down and let them know your coming."

Carrying four cups of coffee on a tray, Boots walked over to the bar and set it down. He looked around for a bar towel so that he could clean the table where Matt and Sierra were sitting. He noticed the silence that echoed in the room, and the feeling of despair emanating from Sierra. He knew that something had happened, something that had brought about this visit. He had an inkling and if it was true the story wasn't going to be pretty. Zack had made it quite clear that they had met Sierra before, in a way that they would never forget.

"Molly will be right down. She said to ask you if you want breakfast. Do you?"

Matt shook his head and Sierra seemed to not hear him.

Molly appeared at the head of the stairs and quickly ascended. She walked over to the table and started lifting the dirty glasses off.

"Gee Boots! Couldn't you have set them down at a clean table?"

"Sure Molly, can you find one?"

"Guess you're right. Some party last night huh?"

As Boots cleaned off the table and then set the coffee in front of each one, Molly walked over and locked the front door.

"Boots tells me that something important is about to happen. Don't want anyone to walk in on us. Now, what's this all about?"

Matt leaned over and took Sierra's hand. He gently lifted it to his lips and kissed it. His eyes met hers and

196

noticing a mist beginning to cover the deep blue depths that he had always gotten lost in, he began:

"There is a story that needs to be told. Sierra has decided that this is the time. She feels that you two need to hear it as well as me."

With three pairs of eyes on her, Sierra raised the coffee cup to her lips and took a sip. Lowering it back to the table she raised her eyes and looked at the people who meant so much to her. She took a deep breath...

Chapter 29

"... I will never tell this story again. It's too painful. But I feel that it's time that the truth comes out. I'm tired of lying and half truths. I don't want to be dishonest or hurt anyone anymore. Please, don't interrupt me. Let me tell it all the way through my way or I might change my mind. Believe me, these memories are a nightmare.

It all started when I was just a small child. I lived here in Wild River Junction with my parents George and Sadie Rathburn. I lived in that farm house you call home Matt. I'm the daughter of the people you called mom and pop. I know they had told you the story of how their only daughter, See See, had been stolen by a man that had worked for them.

I was five years old at the time. I trusted everyone I met. I had never had any reason not to. My parents were such good people and they too trusted any one. Carl had arrived at our doorstep a couple of days prior. He was hungry and looking for work in exchange for food. Pop put him to work right away and mom fed him. He was a good worker and seemed to fit right in with the family. Everything seemed fine. Then it changed. I remember the day it happened as if it was just yesterday.

Carl was going into town on an errand for daddy. I wanted to go. I wanted to see if the new pony that pop had bought me was ready for delivery. I was so excited. Carl had been very pleasant while he worked for pop and after all, what could happen?

We only got a few miles from the farm when Carl turned the wagon off of the usual road and we started to cross over the fields. I remember trying to tell him that he was going the wrong way, but he just laughed. He told me that we were going on a big adventure. We traveled for a long time until we came to the railroad tracks at the water station. It wasn't long before the train came chugging down the tracks. The steam escaping from the big iron horse clouded around my ankles and scared me. I quickly forgot to be scared though as we climbed up the metal steps into the train. The big man with the cap on his head tipped his hat and bowed as I passed him. He told me that he hoped I would have a wonderful trip. In the excitement of our adventure I forgot that we had left the horse and wagon all alone on the prairie or that Mom and Dad wouldn't know where to find me. We rode to the first station. Then Carl got off and purchased tickets and we rode on. For hours we rode. I kept telling him that we had to go back now because mom and dad would be very angry if we were gone too long. It was getting late and I was tired, cold and hungry. Carl told me that mom and pop knew that we would be gone for a long time and for me to stop worrying about it. We finally got off the train. It was very dark out and I had no idea where we were. Carl took my hand and led me over to the local hotel. Not much of a place, and they had no food. That first night was the beginning of my nightmare. There was only one bed in the room and Carl told me that I had to sleep with him. I refused and lay down on the floor. He yanked me up onto the bed and told me that from now on I was to do exactly as he said for me to do or I would get hurt. Then he told me that I wasn't ever going to go home. I was his little girl now and he wouldn't put up with any crying or whining. He said that daddy had sold me to him. I wouldn't let myself believe him and I spent most of the next few days crying. It was only after a whipping from Carl's belt that I dried my tears. After a time I realized that daddy wasn't going to come for me. It was then that I began to believe that what Carl had said was true.

We traveled all over the country one way or another. Sometimes Carl would have money and he would buy a horse and wagon and other times when he was broke he would sell them and we would travel on foot. Lots of times we got a ride from someone traveling in the same direction we were going. If Carl didn't have a plan, we would go wherever the vehicle and driver took us.

One time we spent a year with his brother who lived in Virginia. I shudder every time I remember that place. It was way out in the boonies and I was expected to do all the cooking and cleaning. If I didn't do as I was supposed to I got a good beating with Carl's belt, or got my ears boxed. I had never had that kind of treatment in my life and I couldn't understand what I had done to deserve it. It began to make a coward out of me and I hated the person I had become.

It was toward the end of our living there that I experienced my first sexual encounter. Carl had always been very free with his hands and he had made me do things to him that little girls should not be subjected to. But the actual act of sexual intercourse had not been one of them. He had always" promised" me that someday when I was a women, that he would teach me what true sexual excitement was like. He told me that it would happen on my thirteenth birthday.

I'd been to the creek to bathe on this day. I'd been working in the fields and the temperature had climbed to boiling. I was covered with dirt and dust and my clothes stuck to my body with the sweat that poured out of me. Floating in the water seemed like heaven. Sometimes while doing this I almost felt as if my world wasn't so bad. I had walked into the water fully clothed and as I began to swim around I started to take my clothes off and I threw them up onto the bank hoping they would dry in the sunshine. I knew that I couldn't stay too long or Carl would come looking for me and if he caught me in the water and not doing my nightly chores he would take that dreaded belt off and beat me.

As I walked out of the water Carl's brother was waiting for me. I grabbed at my clothes and started to run, but he was too fast for me. He tackled me to the ground and I fought him with all the strength that a little girl could muster. His rough hands worked their way all over my naked body while he pried my legs apart with his knee. He grabbed hold of both of my wrists with one of his big hands and with the other hand he unbuttoned his breeches and released the terror from within. And while laughing he took me there on the bank of the creek. I screamed and kicked and bit, but he was too big for me to handle. The more I fought him the more excited he became. It was only a few minutes later that it was over. He rolled over onto the ground and shouted with glee. I lay there bleeding and totally horrified. He then rolled on top of me again and said that if I told Carl what he had done he would kill me. After he left I lay there for a long time, not understanding what had happened. When I returned to the cabin that evening Carl was out looking for me. He knew that something had happened and it didn't take him long to guess what it was. He went after his brother and I heard them fighting. It was such fierce sounds, so violent. I ran into the corner of the cabin and sat on the floor with my eyes shut and my hands covering my ears. I never saw his brother again. I don't know what happened to him.

We left the cabin the next day. Carl seemed to be in an awful big hurry to leave. We traveled for days without stopping. I felt that Carl was running from something. After this fight with his brother, Carl became very possessive of me. It wasn't long before he wasn't happy with my role as cook et al.

I was thirteen years old when Carl decided that we should get married. I said no. I didn't want it to happen. But he dragged me in front of one of his hillbilly relatives who was a justice of the peace. The justice pretended that he didn't hear me screaming out 'NO'. He just proceeded with the ceremony and suddenly, I was Carl's wife.

All the years that I was married to Carl, he didn't seem to mind if other men had their way with me. Just as long as he received cash for my work he was happy. Some of the old men were very gentle. Apologized time and again for what they did to me, or what they had me do to them. In one instance unbeknown to Carl, the old man taught me to play piano for my services. Carl would have beaten me silly if he had known. I truly believe that losing myself in the strains of the piano keyboard is the one thing that saved my sanity.

Carl and I had been married about one year when I realized that I was pregnant. I didn't tell him. I was afraid that he would be furious and beat me. I had only one more month to go when Carl came to the realization of why I was getting so fat. He didn't react right away. He just sat there and stared at me. I was so scared. Finally he said that maybe it wouldn't be too bad to have a baby. If it was a girl he would be able to earn twice as much money by putting her to work. It was then that I started praying for a little boy.

My little Annie was born in Virginia. She was such a beautiful baby. I was so proud of her. Carl seemed to be fond of her. I had never forgotten the words that Carl had said before she was born and so I had been salting away every penny that I could beg, borrow or steal. I had a tin box buried in the back of the chicken coup. I just felt that one day Annie and I would be able to get away from Carl. It was on Annie's fourth birthday that I noticed that certain look on Carl's face. He told me that she was sure a pretty little thing. He said that there were lots of men who would pay a fortune to have such a beautiful and young girl. I panicked. I knew that look. I knew what he was planning on doing. Later that night, as Carl sat on the porch drinking himself into a stupor, I knew what I had to do. Very quietly I packed Annie's clothes and mine into a knapsack and stashed it outside the back door. When Carl staggered into the room, he grabbed me by the hair and told me to bring little Annie to him in the bedroom. I couldn't breathe. I would die before I'd let him put his filthy hands on my baby. He fell onto the bed and told me to remove his clothes. I started to unbutton his shirt but he told me to get Annie first. I walked into the kitchen, which was where Annie slept, and as I passed the cook stove I grabbed a piece of firewood. I wrapped a blanket around it and carried it like you carry a child. I entered the bedroom and Carl saw me. He smiled and said bring her over to me. He was having a hard time keeping his eyes open and so I took advantage of it. I pulled the blanket off and raised the wood. As hard as I could I brought it crashing down on Carl's head. I did it again and again. When I finally stopped he was covered in blood. I threw down the wood and ran into the kitchen. I grabbed Annie and the knapsack. Quickly I ran out into the dark night not knowing where I was going or what I would do when I got there. I followed the river bed for days. We ate berries and nuts. Thank goodness the nights were warm. Annie and I would tuck in tight beside the river wherever there was a hollow bank or under a low hanging tree. I kept hearing heavy feet in the underbrush. I was so afraid that Carl was behind us. But it always turned out to be deer coming down to the river to drink.

We walked for days. I had brought along my tin with the little bit of money I had saved. We came across a farm that lay snuggled in the hills alongside the river. It was a pretty little house with a white fence around a beautiful garden. I went around to the back door and knocked. A dear little old lady answered and invited us in. I told her that my husband had died and that we were trying to get to town so that I could get a job to support my baby. She told me that the closest town was twenty miles away and would take a heap of walking to get there. She let us stay with her for a few days and then her son happened to come by to visit with her. He stayed for two days and offered us a ride back to the town where he lived.

When we arrived at the town I got a job in the laundry. While there I met a lady from back east. Her name was Marlene. I'll never forget her. She was the most beautiful woman I had ever seen. Her clothes were made of shimmering materials and the flowers in her hat looked so real. She was so sweet. One day she asked me if I knew how to sew and I told her I did. She brought me a dress that she had torn on a thorn bush and I repaired it for her. She was very excited with the job that I did and so she brought me more mending to do.

One day when she came into the laundry she was very excited. She told me that she was going home to Vermont. I was absolutely devastated. I had come to rely on her and her friendship. She must have sensed how her news had affected me because she smiled and took my hand. Then she said that she would like me to come with her and help her in a new venture she was starting. She was going to open a dress shop for ladies and that the beautiful way I sew would be a great help to her. She said she really needed me and she would be very grateful if I could accompany her. I reminded her about Annie and she said that of course Annie would come too. And that's how I got to Vermont. I spent many happy days there.

After a couple of years Marlene became very ill and had to sell her business. I was heart broken, but realized that I couldn't expect her to be there for me forever. I began to speak to her about opening a shop of my own. She said that she was confident that I would be able to create a successful business. She had presumed that I would stay in Vermont, but I had already decided that I wanted to come home to Wild River. I was anxious to see if there was anything left here for me. You see I had no idea that mom and Pop had died. I didn't even know that I had an adopted brother until I had gone out to the farm and found the old family bible. Yes! That's the reason I have the bible in my shop. I brought it back with me that first day that I went out there. I was very intrigued as to the fact that I had a brother and I wanted to find out about him. Well as you know, I opened the shop. I made friends, and I fell in love. But then, something that I thought would never happen, did happen.

It was at the dance that I saw him. Carl. He knew me right away. I was so scarred I couldn't breathe. He came to my shop later that night and told me that he had been tracking me for years. Always just one step behind. He knew where Annie was living. Our beautiful little Annie he would say. He said that he had talked to Marlene and that was how he had found me. He said that he had told his cousin that if anything happened to him that he was to get Annie and take her to live with him in Virginia. I was so scared. I couldn't let him do to Annie what he had done to me. And when he told me that I was to get my things together and we were leaving town I had no other choice. I had to go with him.

We spent several days out at the farm. He seemed to delight in being there again. He found a lot of enjoyment reminding me of the life I had lived in that house. He thought it very funny that mom and Pop had died still looking for me. He said that if it had been him he would have given up a long time ago. He forced himself on me over and over and would laugh when he was finished. I had no choice. He had me tied to the bed and would only untie my one hand when I ate what little food he prepared. I lived in fear that he would kill me for what I had done to him but I soon realized that he had a far more heinous plan to punish me.

All the time we were at the house he kept telling me that if you were to come out and find us at the farm that he would kill you Matt and how much pleasure that would give him. I was petrified that you would come looking for me. I began to act as if I didn't care about you or Wild River Junction. I told him how I really missed the old days of being on the road, never knowing what lay ahead of us. I think that I almost had him convinced. But he still didn't trust me. Finally he decided that we were leaving the area. As in the past, we again rode to the railroad tracks and got on the train.

We rode as far a Sweet Tree and that's where we moved into the local hotel. He wouldn't let me out of his sight. He said that if I thought I was going to bash his head in again as I had before I had better think again. He said it took him months to get over that beating. Anytime that he went somewhere, I was by his side. Any time that he didn't need me to be with him he would tie me to the bed. If I didn't go along with what he wanted, he would wire his cousin and send him to Vermont to get Annie. I had no choice but to go along with him.

For months I tried to escape from him, to let you all know that I was alright. But to no avail. I remember one time I passed a note to one of the bar tenders in a saloon. I had begged him to get the note to you Molly. I just wanted you to know that I was alright. He read the note and laughed. Carl came over and grabbed the note from his hands. He was furious. I was beaten within an inch of my life that day.

Just as my despair was at its peak, my prayers were answered.

One day in the hall of the hotel a young couple emerged from the room next door to ours. They seemed so happy and excited to be alive. It was very evident that she was expecting a baby very soon. They said hello to Carl and I and Carl bowed and smiled back at them. When we got inside the room, he grabbed me and flung me against the wall and told me that if he ever sees me speaking to either one of those idiot people, he will contact his cousin. I assured him that I had no intentions of speaking to them. Later, thinking about the pregnant lady, it brought back my time with Annie. Although I was so young and had no knowledge as to the process of childbirth, I had born her with no help from Carl or anyone. I only hoped that the woman would have an easier time of it.

It was late one evening. Carl and I were in our room. Suddenly there was a pounding on the door. Carl jumped up and grabbed his gun. Heaven only knows who he thought it was. He yelled out for the caller to identify himself. It was the young man from next door. He was in a panic. His wife was in labor and he had to go to find the doctor and he didn't want to leave her alone. He begged Carl to let me sit with her. He promised it would be just for a few minutes. Carl struggled with this request and I knew better than to try to talk him into it. Finally Carl hollered through the door that if his wife did this that the man was to pay him for it.

The man was so beside himself with worry that he agreed. Carl pulled on my arm and warned me that if I tried anything stupid I would pay for it. I acknowledged the fact that I understood. Carl opened the door and I slipped from our room into our neighbor's room.

She was lying on the bed with the quilts up around her. Her pale face told me that she had been in labor for a while. Quietly she thanked me for coming in. She told me that the doctor had previously instructed them as to what supplies they were to have on hand when her time came and the implements were all lined up on the night table waiting for the doctor's skilled hands to use them. She was suddenly wracked by a violent contraction. I grabbed her hand and helped her through it. She asked if I had ever had a baby and of course I said that I had and that she was staying with friends in the east while my husband and I were traveling. It seemed forever before the doctor got there and when he did he asked the father to leave the room, but asked if I would stay to help. He determined that it would be hours before the baby would come, in fact, it seems that her body had stopped the birthing process. He announced that he would come back in a couple of hours and would appreciate my help at that time. The doctor left to speak to the husband in the hallway. When he shut the door, the woman closed her eyes and seemed to drift off into a light slumber.

I remember staring at the implements. My eyes wouldn't leave the sharp knife that was laying there. I was mesmerized. It was to be used to cut the umbilical cord. Then I heard the door handle quietly turn and as the husband entered I quickly slipped the knife into the folds of my skirt. I told him to let me know when she continued her labor and I would come right over. Then I walked out of their room and into mine.

Carl was sleeping when I entered. He was loudly snoring with his mouth wide open. He was a hairy creature sprawled out on the bed. A really beautiful sight to behold he was. This was always the way he ended up at the end of the day. It was the effects of the alcohol he had been consuming all day.

I paced the floor. What did I think I was going to do with the knife? If I killed him I would hang. I couldn't let that happen. That would leave Annie all alone. Besides if he died his cousin might find out and then Annie would be in danger. I must think my plan very carefully.

He awoke with a grunt. He asked why I was there instead of next door. I told him. Again he warned me about slipping away from him. He then thought that because we had some time on our hands that I should pleasure him for a while. I quickly poured him another large shot of whiskey and before he had finished drinking it he had passed out again

While Carl slept, I paced. I tried planning what to do, how to get away from him. My mind didn't seem to want to face this situation. Whatever I did had to be done with the upmost of care so as not to hurt Annie. Suddenly Carl woke up. He sat up and with his hairy legs dangling over the edge of the bed he grinned. He told me that he had decided we were going to Vermont and get Annie. After all, he said, she was his daughter. Besides, there was no sense wasting all this time playing my game. He wanted her here with him. He had to make more money somehow and having her with him would make it easier to get. He told me that he knew a lot of men that would pay a fortune to have a young innocent child for the first time.

I screamed at him. I told him that he couldn't do that. The anger flared in his eyes and he jumped up from the bed and grabbed me by the hair. His hand quickly flew through the air and struck me on the check. He screamed that I had no choice in this matter. I was to do exactly as he said or I would be sorry. Besides, he added, its time that little Annie started earning her keep.

My rage engulfed me from head to toe. I turned around and thrashed out at Carl. He only laughed as he hit me again. His face showed surprise when I suddenly found a strength I never knew that I had. I pushed him hard onto the bed and as he landed, I pulled the knife from the folds of my skirt and thrust the knife into his chest again and again. He didn't even cry out. I didn't care if I was caught. I just wanted to be sure that my Annie would always be safe.

I stood back and looked at his still body. There was no remorse. I had done what I needed to do. A cool calm seeped into my body and I could feel it creeping inside every pore. It was over. No more fear. The monster that had taken my life from me was no longer. He was dead. A joy came bubbling up from inside of me. I began to laugh and laugh and laugh.

Then at that same instance there came a pounding on the door. It was the man from the next room. "Hurry he screamed, there is no time for the doctor now." I shouted back to him that I would be right there and quickly I pulled the knife from Carl's chest and wiped it on my skirt. I saw that my apron was speckled with blood so I pulled it over my head and turned it inside out hoping that no one would notice it. I calmly walked over to the door, took one more look at the form on the bed to be sure that my demon was gone and I walked out of the room and entered my neighbor's room.

The poor little thing! She looked so small and white and was in so much pain. It was evident that she was in the last throes of her labor and I could see the crown of the baby's head. I sent her husband to get some warm water and some clean rags, and then I proceeded to bring a beautiful baby girl into this world. This must have been one of God's plans. One had died and one was born. Please God I prayed don't ever let her know the pain that I have had to live with.

Within the hour, little Marie was all washed, bundled up and in her mother's arms. One of the mysteries of childbirth is the fact that there is no pain more intense and yet it is the pain that is the quickest forgotten. After being sure that his wife and daughter were comfortable the father had taken the necessary implements, including the knife, into the bathroom down the hall. He washed them and then put them away.

What a happy couple they were. Yes Boots it was your son and his wife that I helped that day.

As I walked out of the room, the doctor arrived and we stood in the hallway talking for a few minutes about the birth. While talking I untied my apron and rolled it into a ball. It had come in contact with the blood from the birthing and was unsalvageable. There was no way anyone could tell that some of the blood on it was Carl's. I hesitated for a moment outside my room. I was waiting for the doctor to go to the new mother and baby.

As I reached to open the door, the doctor, being the gentlemen that he was, offered to help me. I jumped, startled, not wanting him to see what was waiting for me in the room. But, it was too late. He turned the knob and the door opened just a slit, then it stopped, it had hit something. He pushed and pushed and then finally he was able to look around the door and he saw the body of Carl, lying on the floor. Evidently he had been able to drag himself off of the bed and over as far as the door before he finally died. When I realized what had happened, I screamed, loudly. Not from grief, as the doctor thought, but from relief.

When the sheriff came he couldn't understand what had happened to the murder weapon. He said that the killer must have taken it with him. They all said that I was so lucky not to have been in the room when the murderer came in. Probably, they decided, someone that Carl had cheated at cards. I guess that Carl had a bad reputation for never playing an honest game.

After we buried Carl, the sheriff gave me permission to leave town. After all, how could I have had anything to do with Carl's death when I was delivering a baby at that same moment?

It only took me a very short time to put my things to-gether and that was when I came back here. I only wanted to live my life here with all of you. I didn't even want to think about the terrible thing that I had done. But now that you know Matt, I guess that you'll have to arrest me for murder. After all this is my confession and you are a sworn officer of the law.

Chapter 30

There hadn't been a sound during the telling of Sierra's story. The three listeners had sat in stunned silence. Each one of them was reflecting their emotions in their eyes. Disbelief! Horror! Sadness! The story of this beautiful woman had been full of terrible things that no one should have to go through. How could she have survived as long as she did?

"Matt, now you know why I couldn't tell you the truth. I knew that it would be the end of our relationship. There would not be a future for us when you knew what I had done. But in my heart I'm glad that I told you. I just couldn't go on lying any more. What are we going to do now?"

"Right now Sierra I think I'm going to go over to the office. You've given me a lot to think about. Molly, will you see that Sierra gets home."

Not looking anywhere in particular, Matt walked out the door of the saloon and disappeared.

Molly was dumfounded. She looked directly at Boots, her mouth open in shock. Her eyes wide to their fullest and she gasped the air into her lungs.

"What in the hell is wrong with him? What on earth made him walk out of here without a word? Good God Sierra, you did what you had to do. You did what anyone else, myself included, would have done. Only I probably would have done it sooner than you did. What a mean son-of-a-bitch. Don't just sit there Boots, say something to her. She wasn't in the wrong."

"I know Molly. I find it so hard to comprehend that any man could treat another human being in that way. My God! Taking her away at such a young age and submitting her to all the degradation in the world. Sierra I just don't know what to say to you. I am so stunned. I only know that I believe you to be one of the best people I know. Look what you did for my son and daughter-in-law. How could I ever think something bad of you? You had every right to get kill him."

Sierra looked long and hard at her two dear friends. She found it hard to speak. There seemed to be a lump in her throat that made her voice quiver.

"Thank you, both of you. I don't really know what to do right now, except that I think I should send a wire to Arletta and tell her that I won't be coming for Annie right now. I have to figure out what's going to happen. If Matt arrests me then I sure don't want Annie here."

The confusion that showed on Sierra's face was only complicated by the disappointment she felt. What had she expected? Matt couldn't just wash everything away. He was a sworn officer of the law and bound to uphold any crime that he was aware of. In anyone's book, murder was a crime.

"Sierra, come on and I'll walk with you to the telegraph office and then we'll come back here and you can use my apartment for a while. I don't want you to be alone. I know that Matt will figure something out. He wouldn't desert you. He loves you too much. I bet he's figuring out a way that will make everything work. It may take time, but he'll do it."

"Yeah, you're probably right Molly. I was just scared when I saw the look on his face. I wasn't sure just what I was seeing in his eyes."

All three of them pushed away from the table and as Sierra walked passed Boots, he pulled her to him and held her very gently. Without saying a word, she knew that at least in his eyes she was not to blame for what happened. When he let her go, he turned and Molly could see the tears that were in his eyes. She leaned over and put her arms around his neck and kissed him.

"There are times that I cannot understand you men." Molly said, "But there are times that I like to see the softer side of you."

As Molly and Sierra walked out into the quiet street they saw a rider in the distance. He seemed to be in a hurry guiding his horse on the trail out of town.

"Molly! That looks like Matt's horse. Where's he going? Oh dear God, I have ruined everything. What can I do? I feel as if my life is over."

"Now don't be so stupid Sierra. Your life is not over. Look at what you have accomplished in spite of your horrific beginning. You have a beautiful little girl that is just waiting to come and live with you. I promise you that Matt will find a way to make this right. But you can't fall apart over it. Not now. Maybe when it's all settled you can, but not right now. You have to keep your wits about you."

"Yes, your right Molly. Lets hurry and get the telegram sent and maybe Matt will be back by then. And one thing I just thought about. When I send that telegram to Arletta, I must be sure and tell her not to let anyone else take Annie. If Carl was telling the truth about his cousin, then he might try to get her when he hears that Carl is dead. I wouldn't be able to bear that. I always suspected that Carl killed his brother that time they had that fight because I never heard of him again, but if he's alive I can't take any chances."

"Sounds like a good plan to me Sierra. On our way back we'll stop by the sheriff office and see if Matt is back."

They proceeded down the street saying very little to each other. Their own minds were crowded with thoughts of what had been divulged that day. Molly was so certain that

214

Matt would rise to the occasion and Sierra so apprehensive as to his decision.

When they returned to the saloon they told Boots about seeing Matt leave town. They had stopped by the office, but it was locked up tight. The two women walked up to Molly's rooms and settled in. Molly put a bottle of brandy on the table and two glasses. She poured a good stiff shot into each glass and raised her drink up high. A toast, she felt was in order.

"Here is to you and Matt. Your lives have just begun and I want you to believe that too."

"Thank you Molly. I appreciate all that you have done for me. I have one more favor to ask. When I am arrested and put in prison, would you consider taking Annie and raising her here, as your own child?"

"Good grief woman. That won't be necessary. You'll have her yourself before too long. I'll be here to baby sit her anytime you want, but don't think for one moment that she won't grow up without you."

If only I could believe that, Sierra thought. The sight of Matt riding away only added to the anxious feelings that his attitude had brought forth.

* * * *

Sierra decided to move back into her own little place after waiting three days for Matt to return. She received no word from him. No gossip was heard as to where he had gone. Nobody seemed to know. Even his deputy knew only that Matt had left town in a hurry and he had no idea when he would be back. She was totally in the dark and so apparently was the whole town. She decided not to open the shop. What would be the use if Matt came back and took her away? She would take inventory or something mundane as that. She must do something to keep busy. Maybe she should start packing some of the things away. Mr. Bellman at the General Store would probably buy some of her merchandise. There was a lot that he could sell. Well, most of it anyway. How she would miss the shop. It had brought her such a lot of happiness over the past months. It was something that she had created with her own two hands, and was totally hers. Just like Annie. But she couldn't think about her right now. She would have to wait and find out what the future held.

Molly came by to see her over the next few days. She was trying to keep Sierra's spirits up. Molly still trusted the fact that Matt would come up with an answer. But as the time went by and still no word from Matt, Sierra found it harder to believe. She thought sometimes that she should just run away. Then she knew that she couldn't do that. It wouldn't solve anything. She'd just stay and face whatever was in store.

One Sunday morning she felt as if she was going stir crazy. She had been closed up inside for days now. A desire for some fresh air got the best of her. She just felt she needed a change of scenery. She wandered down to the livery stable and asked Gabe to hitch up a wagon for her. She said she would be going on a picnic and be gone most of the day. Quickly he had the wagon ready to go and he watched her ride out of town. He knew that something had happened between Matt and Sierra. He just didn't know what and no matter how much he questioned Molly and Boots, he couldn't get any answers.

There had been some pretty deep discussions between Molly and Boots. They had rehashed Sierra's story over and over again. They had been so astounded at the cruelty of the man that had controlled her life.

"I can only thank God that she was able to get away from him and was able to keep that baby away from him. None of us ever know to what depths we will go to survive situations like that. Just think, Boots, at least she was at the right time and place for your son and his wife. What a beautiful baby they have. We might never have known the truth if Zack hadn't decided to come to Wild River."

"Yes, we might never have known. But – would that have been a bad thing? Not to know I mean. Sierra would have been back east right now getting her baby ready for the return trip and we would all know where Matt was. They would have had a great life. How quickly things go wrong in our lives. I know when I lost my family it was in the blink of an eye. We should all jump at the chance of happiness. If it doesn't work out, well at we least we tried."

"Of course, you're right. We always wait for something better to happen instead of taking the happiness of the moment. Why are we afraid that we'll be rejected? Why is that do you suppose?"

"I don't know Molly old girl. One thing I do know is that I have wasted way too much time keeping my thoughts and feelings to myself. I'm always afraid I might be rejected by the person that means the most to me but by golly I'm not going to do that any longer.

Boots walked over to Molly and gently taking her hand he lifted it to his lips and kissed her palm. Then lifting his head he looked deep into her eyes. He realized that this was the right time.

"Molly, I adore you, I love you with all my heart. I have respected and admired you since the first time I saw you. You gave me a new chance at life and saw to it that I lived it. We've been good friends for years now, and I feel that you maybe, could love me. Am I right?"

"You are very wrong Boots. It's not that I could love you; it's that I do love you. I finally realized it a few weeks ago although I believe that I loved you long before that. I kept finding you on my mind and I missed you when you weren't around me. I would watch for you and then breathe a sigh of relief when you walked into the room. I've felt like a young girl whose heart flitter flatters just looking at you. Oh yes, my dear Boots. I love you with all my heart."

"Then I think it's time we did something about this relationship don't you? I believe that we should get married. We have a good chance of living happily ever after. What do you say Molly? Marry me?"

Boots was surprised to see tears glistening in Molly's eyes. Were they tears of joy? To Molly they were. A whole lifetime of wishes seemed to be coming true at this special moment. She didn't hesitate with her reply to Boots.

"The first moment that this mess with Sierra is straightened out I will be proud to marry you Boots and the sooner the better as far as I am concerned. I can't wait. Oh Boots, how can I feel so happy knowing how unhappy Sierra is? It doesn't seem fair."

"It isn't fair, but I think we should keep this news between ourselves for now. We can tell Matt and Sierra when they're together again. Now come here and let's seal our decision with a real kiss. No more pecks on the checks my love."

She came to him slowly and watched his eyes. A man's soul shines through his eyes she had always been told. If that's true then I see a bright shiny soul in my future. Gently, and hesitantly she raised her lips to his. This had to be something special, this first kiss. It would be something that they would always remember.

Chapter 31

Even though she hadn't given it any thought before she started Sierra knew where she would end up. The farm drew her to it like a magnet.

Where else could she be close to those that she had loved and that had loved her. Maybe they were gone now, but she could still feel their presence all around her. Her footsteps echoed in the house and the thin layer of dust that lay about couldn't diminish things that were vivid in her memory.

The old black pot was still hanging over the fireplace. She could almost smell the essence of the food in the cauldron; hear the bubbling of the juices. How wonderful on a cold winter day to run back into the house after spending time with her father in the fields after helping him fix the fences or track down one of the lambs that had strayed away from the sheep pen. When the cold air bit at your fingertips and nipped your nose you just knew that it was getting closer to the end of the day and you couldn't wait to return to the house. Mom would be waiting for us with a warm fire in the kitchen and tonight's dinner on the stove. If we were lucky, there would be hot biscuits in the oven, and maybe even a pie. My favorite of all was mom's cherry pie. She would pick the cherries from the two cherry trees that she and dad had planted the first year they lived on the farm. Were the trees still there, Sierra wondered? Was it possible that people could be as happy as the three of us had been before...? Was it possible that people could be that naive? How could we have been so blind as to trust Carl when he came into our lives? I should have talked to mom about some of the conversations that I'd had with Carl. I knew at the time they happened that they made me feel very uncomfortable but I didn't know why. Maybe I was so afraid that she would say that I must have been bad for him to say those things to me. Never in my short life did I believe that he would hurt me. Was I ever wrong? Looking back it was easy to see what should have been done. At that time, it was just something you don't believe could possibly happen.

Wandering through the house Sierra could see where Matt had been working. He had added another room onto the side of the kitchen. It was to be Annie's bedroom. She was to have a room all to herself. He wanted it there because he felt that it would be warmer for her in the winter time to be close to the fireplace. He was almost finished with it. All it really needed were the panes of glass in the windows. I had ordered the fabric for the curtains and it should be here any day now. Matt was going to build her a bed and bring one of the old dressers down from the attic. He wanted to paint it all to match. Nothing but the best for Annie he had told her.

Looking out of the window of Annie's room Sierra saw a young fawn standing munching on the greenery. As she watched he bent his front legs and lowered his body onto the grass. He looked so small and you could hardly see him amongst the tall waving blades. He had just a few spots on his back. His mother must be around someplace. She wouldn't leave him alone. How safe he must feel. I hope that they come back when Annie is here, she will love them so.

She turned from the window and walked back through the kitchen, passed the table and chairs and entered the room on the opposite side. It had been mom and pops room. She and Matt had spent time in here getting the room ready for when they would be living here as husband and wife. The enormous bed stood with its four posters almost touching the ceiling. She remembered that pop had been a big man and he always said that he needed a big bed in order to stretch out at night and not be keeping mom awake. Mom said that his legs walked as much when he was asleep as they did during the day. Sierra walked over to the bed and ran her hand over the quilts that gave a colorful hue to the room. She watched as the sunlight beamed down from the window onto the spread. Mom had made these quilts. She and several of the women in town had formed a quilt club and they met once a week. Each one of them worked on their own creations. Mom said that visiting with the other ladies helped make the time go by faster and she seemed to get more sewing work done. She was also able to keep up with the local gossip. What a joyous day when mom had laid the quilt on top of their bed. Pop made a big production about it. He was so proud of anything that mom accomplished. He said he had no doubt that they had the most beautiful quilt in the state – even in the country. That first morning afterward, pop announced that he had never in his life slept so peacefully or so warm. Mom had been so happy he took such notice of her handiwork. But then, that was how Pop was. He appreciated everything and everyone.

Sierra sat down on the side of the bed. It creaked just a little. From old age, she had no doubt. "I'd creak too if I was as old as this bed," she thought. It was so soft and comfortable. Before she realized it she had laid her head down on the pillow. They were only covered in ticking right now, but had been aired and cleaned well. The new pillowcases that she had made would look so good. She had even embroidered her and Matt's initials on them. She had MBR on one and SRR on the other. That stood for Matthew Barnes Rathburn and Sierra Rose Rathburn. A mist of tears filled her eyes as she remembered how happy she had been when she was making them. She had been so full of hope for the future. Only now, that was all over. She had no idea where Matt was. He had left her so quickly and was gone before she could understand what had happened. But she knew what had happened. After he had heard her story, he was horrified and couldn't bear to look at her. She was after all a murderer. She had deliberately killed a human being. But Carl wasn't human. He was the devil himself. No matter how hard I try I cannot feel remorse for what I did. I only hope that God will forgive me when I meet him. Maybe he will understand what Matt couldn't. With this thought she closed her eyes and slipped off into a peaceful slumber.

The sounds of a horse galloping into the yard woke Sierra with a start. How long had she been asleep? She jumped off the bed and ran to the door well aware that she had no way of protecting herself from whoever it was. It was nearing dusk and a couple of stars twinkled in the sky. Her panic subsided when she saw the rider. It was Matt. She gasped and started shaking. "Thank God he is safe," she said aloud.

When he saw her standing in the doorway he reined his horse in and dismounted. For one brief second he stood there, taking in the wondrous sight of the women that he had married. Was it only a few days ago?

What he saw in her eyes broke his heart. With quick strides he was reaching for her. He took her in his arms and held her tight declaring never to let her go.

"Oh Sierra, my love. I'm so sorry I've been gone for so long. I didn't mean to leave you like that, but I couldn't figure out any other way. All I could think of was to find some strategy that would help me to save you. Please forgive me. I love you so much and it pains me to see the hurt look in your eyes."

With this he kissed her urgently and long.

Sierra felt her heart leap. He loved her! He still loved her! Dear God in heaven he was here beside her again and she could feel the warmth of his body next to hers. She couldn't stem the flow of tears from her eyes anymore than she could stop the feeling of relief that swept over her.

Sierra felt that her heart would burst with love for this man. He didn't hate her after all. Molly had said that he would figure out a way. She matched his enthusiasm with her own and before they realized it they were locked together in a passion that surpassed their wildest imagination. He lifted her into his arms and carried her into their bedroom. Gently he laid her on the oversized bed. His lips had never left hers for an instance and he quickly undressed her. The big bed reverberated to the rhythm of their passion and the climax to their coupling came amid shouts of joy, pain and ecstasy. Their passion spent Matt turned to Sierra and kissed her again softly this time.

* * * *

"I know I have a lot to explain as to where I've been and what happened, and I will. But will you trust me for just a few more hours. Can we just lie here and enjoy each other? I've ridden night and day to get here and I was terrified when I couldn't find you. I had visions of you disappearing again. I'm exhausted. Please just let me hold you and rest for a while."

"Matt, now that you're back I don't care if you never tell me what happened. I trust you. I should have trusted you more. Molly said I was a fool not to. She was so right. She knows you better than I do."

"Tomorrow you will hear what happened. Just let me rest tonight."

Matt pulled Sierra into his arms and he laid his head on the pillow. It was only moments before Sierra could feel the regular shallow breathing of her sleeping lover. She half turned and watched him. His chest rose and fell with each breath. She closed her eyes and enjoyed the essence of him beside her. The tranquility that surrounded her crept into her very existence.

"Dear God! Please let this be real. Not a dream" She thought. Then with the gentle echo of their two heartbeats she slowly slipped away into a very good place.

The tip of the sun was rising over the far hills when they awoke. They both wondered if this was a dream, but then realized that it was real.

The wonder of waking to find the one you love lying next to you was unbelievable. The urgency of the chemistry pulled at them as they, again, explored each other's body. Such elation must be the wonders of the love that they had always heard about. With dual climatic response, they pounded out their desire. The release was unfathomable. Such ravaging motions and suddenly - calm and peace. The coupling of husband and wife had been satiated for a moment. But they knew that the desire would soon return again.

"Sierra, would you mind if we get dressed and go back into town. I know that Molly and Boots are waiting for us. I saw them yesterday when I was looking for you and I told them that if I found you I would explain after I had brought you back. Of course, if you want me to explain to you before we go, I could do that."

"No Matt. I don't need your explanation. I'll accept whatever it is you have decided to do. I owe a lot to Molly and I want to include her in this. Let's go and meet Boots and Molly. I don't want to cause her any more worry. I've given her enough reason to do that in the past."

Hitching up his horse behind the wagon, Matt grabbed the reins and drove Sierra into town. They didn't hurry this trip. They wanted to relish the happiness that they both felt. The gentle clip clop of the horse's hooves as they hit the ground seemed to keep in time with Sierra's heart beat. The sun was rising over the hill and its warmth seeped into their bones. It would have been so easy to just close her eyes and drift back into the dream world that she had visited during the early hours of the morning. It seemed like such a short time before the steeple of the church rose up above the hillside and they knew that they were coming into Wild River Junction. The horse seemed to know he was heading home to a clean stable and a fine meal. He took his head and the reins couldn't dissuade his from his journey. A quick turn here and another turn there and the saloon was in front of them. Pulling to a stop Matt ran around the wagon and lifted Sierra down onto the wooden sidewalk. No sooner had they taken three steps when the swinging doors banged open and both Molly and Boots were standing there.

"Thank God Matt. I was starting to worry about you both. I thought that you hadn't found her after you left here."

"Sorry Molly. She was exactly where I had thought she would be. It just took us a while to get re-acquainted." Matt said with a broad grin on his face. He looked at Sierra and she was trying to hide a sly smile.

"Darn it all Molly. I told you that you shouldn't worry about them. After all they're married people now. What they do when they're together is none of your business. Honest Matt, I spent most of the night trying to calm her down which wasn't such a terrible chore." Boots grinned at this statement and gave Molly a wink.

"Well come in you two and let's get this thing settled once and for all. I've got a pot of coffee waiting. We can eat afterwards. I'll lock the door for a while so that we won't be interrupted. I'm going to be out of business at this rate if I don't stop locking all my customers outside each time we get together."

The four friends walked across the floor to a table that Molly had set with coffee mugs. A bottle of her best whiskey had been set in the middle of the table with four sparkling glasses surrounding it. She was hoping that Sierra and Matt could clear up their problem so that she and Boots could tell them of their decision to marry. Molly was very anxious to make the announcement but she also felt very ashamed of being so selfish. "Guess that's what love does to you," she thought. Hopefully there would be a toast to all four of them soon.

Chapter 32

"I want you to understand Sierra that I was absolutely shocked by what you told us. Not about the ending (heaven knows you were totally justified in your action), but at the story that led up to it. I couldn't fathom the depth of the abuse you had suffered.

I want you to remember I was living with mom and Pop. I know the sadness that was always there when your name was mentioned or if they came across something that had been yours. There was one time in particular that Pop came across an old doll in the barn. There had been a slat loose and Pop decided to nail it back in place. He moved a bunch of old worn out tools away from where he was going to work, and then suddenly I heard him cry out. I didn't know what had happened and by the time I got to him he was sitting down on the ground holding something that was dirty and covered with cob webs. He was sobbing his heart out and just looking at the object. As I got closer I recognized it as a doll. After a while he pulled himself together and told me that it had been See See's doll. Your doll! He said that you were always hiding your dolls. You would pretend that you were the sheriff and you would look for these children and then return them to their mommies and daddies. He said he had told you that a lady doesn't become a sheriff and you had announced quite loudly that by golly you were going to become one when you grew up even if you were the first lady to do it.

Anyway, as time passed, the hurt didn't seem to get any better for them. I asked them one time if they had searched for you. They told me that they had spent all the money they had been able to save searching for you. There had been a lot of people that claimed that they had seen you with someone that looked like Carl. Pop would then hire someone to go and search for you in whatever direction the informant had told Pop that he thought you were last seen. Pop asked them to bring back any information they might get. All of them insisted on being paid up front. Some were honest people and brought back news that was of no help, but most of them never came back again. They lost a lot of money that way. It seemed that their See See, Sierra, had totally disappeared.

It was of one of these leads that caused mom and pop to race into town that day.

There was a certain drifter who told someone in the saloon that he had seen Carl with a young girl. The rumor that he had seen you had reached pop through one of his neighbors. Pop found out that the drifter was leaving town that day and if they wanted the information they would have to hurry. Pop didn't want the drifter to get away before they had a chance to speak to him.

When they left the farm they were so excited. They both had such high expectations that this time it would lead them to you. Hope sure can drive a body on. Pop knew better than to urge speed out of his horses. He was always lecturing me about being very cautious when driving the team. But that day he threw caution to the wind and that was the day that their wagon overturned and both of them were killed

After you told me your story Sierra, I panicked. I knew that I had to get beyond the fact that you had confessed to murder. You are my wife and I couldn't bear the thought of you going to prison. I needed time to think. I had to work out some kind of a plan to help you. So my answer to do this was to go off and leave you with no explanation as to why I reacted like that. Doesn't say much for me as a man does it?

Sitting in my office I was suddenly very ashamed. I decided that the only decent thing I could do would be to go to you and beg your forgiveness.

As I stood up behind my desk I noticed that without thinking about it I had been toying with a wanted poster that was on my desk. I didn't really see it cause my mind was on more important things, but suddenly a certain word jumped out at me. I then read the poster. I couldn't believe what I was reading. Could this be true? There was only one way for me to find out. I grabbed the poster and ran out the door. I jumped on my horse and headed out of town. This was going to be settled one way or the other.

I rode over to Sweet Tree. It was a long hard ride. It took me a couple of days. But I didn't stop. My poor horse was exhausted when we rode into town. I found the Sheriff's office and imagine my surprise when I found out he was an old friend of mine. Sheriff Bryan Childers. Neither of us had any knowledge of the other being involved with the law. I didn't want to bring up the subject of the poster right away; I wanted to make it seem casual. No sense in tipping my hand. I didn't want to explain why I was interested in the wanted man. We talked a little about our lives and he told me about Sweet Tree. Seems it's an up and coming place to live. Now that the railroad comes through they're able to transport the cattle to market without having to drive them hundreds of miles. We ended the evening by walking around the shops in town and checking the doors. He was right. It was a nice town. Kept clean and lots of shops to create business that would bring new people into town. We ended up in the hotel restaurant. Sitting in that place had me remembering what you had said about Carl keeping you locked up in a room upstairs, abusing you. My being in the same place that he had been, made my hair stand on end.

After a really fine dinner, we adjourned into the lobby of the hotel. We had a glass of brandy and smoked a cigar. Finally I asked him if there had been many killings in Sweet

Tree. He told me that every once in a while some drunken cow poke would get all fired up about who knows what and shoot someone. Of the couple of shootings that had occurred only one of the people had died. That was several years ago. Then he told me that he had almost forgotten about a death that had occurred in the hotel just a couple of months ago. It seems that a certain man had been playing poker at saloons and gambling houses all over town. He became very well known as a card shark and was accused of cheating everyone he played against. Evidently word had got out about him and his name was put on a hit list. Everyone wanted him dead, but no one wanted to take the chance of being caught.

Well, one evening, two men came into the hotel looking for him. He had been in his room sleeping off a day of drinking. The clerk gave them the number of the room that Carl and his wife were staying in. They evidently went upstairs and found the door unlocked so they burst into the room. Carl, this guy, was lying on the bed and one of the men said that he looked like he was sleeping. But then suddenly Carl had sat up and had muttered something that they couldn't understand. They could only think it sounded like wife – or life – something like that. They dragged him off the bed and took turns stabbing him. Then, leaving his body against the door on the carpeted floor, they jumped out of the window, landed on a veranda that ran all the way around the hotel then ran down the stairs. My friend said that it was a lucky thing that Carl's wife wasn't in the room. She might have been murdered too. Evidently she was in the next room helping a woman give birth. It was about a month later that they found out about these two men. They had both been bragging around town as to what they had done. Unfortunately, or I think we should say fortunately, one of them had escaped. The one in custody had confessed to the sheriff the whole story of what happened. It seems that both of them had been drinking all day trying to build up their courage. I guess that Carl had cheated them both out of a lot of money.

The flyer that I'd found lying on my desk was the wanted poster for the second man. When I read it, I couldn't believe it. If he had never escaped there would not have been a flyer issued on him. That's why I had to find out the truth before I came back here and told you.

Don't you see Sierra? You didn't kill Carl. You may have wounded him, but these two men finished the job for you. Your safe my love. Our lives are going to be just as we planned. You, me and Annie."